I0517129

Grey Cat Blues

J.D. Cowan

Thanks to L. Jagi Lamplighter, Declan Finn, Brian Niemeier, Jeffro Johnson, Kukuruyo, and everyone else I am forgetting.

This book was made possible thanks to you.

Chapter 1
"Howling Downpour"

Tonight was a good night for Two Tone. Outside the bar, the rain beat endlessly against the old brick, and the clouds masked the dual moons of Achaea. It fit in well with the old, familiar, crumbling city of Cordova on the planet of Achaea. But tonight was different. Tonight Two Tone was with a friend.

The two of them went on about the old days, an ancient time when the gangs were still around, and you could punch some hound in the teeth for looking at you cross-eyed. That was a lifetime ago. The chaos eventually destroyed Cordova, though the menace still hung in the atmosphere like the sword of Damocles even so many years later. The city was a shell of what it could have been.

But his friend didn't see it that way. A-Rail was there to relive a past that was long gone. He always had Two Tone's back in the old days, but that was a long time ago. Two Tone was happy to see his old friend again, but preferred the past stay buried. Still, Jet Boys were always there for each other.

"You don't get it," A-Rail mumbled. He punched Two Tone's shoulder, and almost fell out of his seat doing so. "No, cat, you've got it made."

"Bull." Two Tone took a drink from his water glass. "I work for a creep who was arrested more times than we were back in the day, stalks his ex-wife, and whispers perverted jokes to himself when he thinks no one is in earshot. That doesn't sound so great to me."

"Sounds like a real hound. But at least you've got a job."

"It doesn't matter." Two Tone stretched his arms. "We're going to be replaced with an automated system soon enough. Almost everyone there works from home except me."

"We're all going to be replaced," A-Rail said, glumly.

Two Tone cocked an eyebrow. "Huh?"

"Nothing."

"You heard about the attacks around town? People have been disappearing. Know anything about the gang behind it?"

"I heard some of the guys got involved. But I haven't seen 'em in years. The sooner I get out of Cordova the better."

"You still talk to Jet or Martin? It's been awhile. Used to practice throwing knives with Jet. Haven't done it in ages."

"Jet's dropped off the map. I think he still lives in the Grove, but I don't go over there. Martin still hangs with Scotty, and he's still deep into Rocks. Wouldn't surprise me if either of them have anything to do with whatever's causing cats to vanish."

Martin and Scotty were friends from way back. There

were few things less believable than Martin going out of his way to harm anyone—he was a quiet guy, didn't stick out in a crowd, and kept to himself. Despite his good build, he didn't stick out in a crowd. Scotty was the same, but he was a talker and not as big as Martin. He was always on the hunt for a kitten to hang with. How those two ever got along was anyone's guess.

"I don't know about that," Two Tone said. "The guys could be hounds, but they weren't far gone. But that was then. The rest of the Jet Boys left town, as far as I know. We all gotta move on. Fair enough for them."

It felt like a lifetime ago when Two Tone ran with the gang. They were all idealistic kids watching each other's backs and made of tougher stuff. Jet was tougher than anyone. A-Rail was the brains, and Two Tone was the mediator between them. But it wasn't all fighting. Evan was a lady's man and introduced Two Tone to his first girl, Alice. Scotty was a daredevil and did just about anything for some attention. Martin read a lot and was the one who got Two Tone thinking about Earth. Alby was the only other guy who used to spar with Jet other than Two Tone. They were a weird bunch. But that was almost another life.

"How long has been since Marble Gates?" Two Tone whispered.

A-Rail growled. "Why do you have to bring that up? Of all the things to remember, you pick when Evan died?"

"Should I have picked something more pleasant? How about the Viper Coil incident or Stagger Lee trying to buy us out? Do you remember the time I had glass taken out of my arm? The fight where you almost lost an eye? How about when Scotty stole Jet's girl and was beaten into the dirt? It was great, A-Rail. Really. I loved those days. At the time. Now I just want to live the rest of my days out alone and not to be reminded of how it was all for nothing."

"You were never this stupid."

"No, I was even dumber. How many of you guys still work for Stagger Lee, anyway? Were you bought in by the rumors?"

"They're not rumors, cat. He shot someone and the bullet disappeared. The man's creepy."

"I'll tell you what's creepy," Two Tone began, careful to keep his voice low. "I'm not sure if it's the atmosphere here on Achaea, or something the planet did to us for living here for so long, but I keep hearing there are people with strange mental abilities. Like bending spoons or whatever."

"In Cordova?"

"No, we'd know about that. In one of the hundreds of other cities. Who knows what's out there."

"Not you. You're retired and want to be left alone like a damn hermit."

"At least I don't engage in alien theories. You still think the little green men are coming, A-Rail?"

"Well, I can tell you we aren't alone out here, even if we're the only intelligent thing on this ball of mud. And at least I'm not a loner freak."

Two Tone cocked his head, curious. "What's wrong with wanting to be alone? I'm not hurting anyone."

"We're not all satisfied with living like hobos, Two Tone.

Some of us want a bit more from life."

"You want more from life? Try drinking real liquor instead of beer, pussy. We're still in our twenties, not old men."

"Funny."

Two Tone laughed. "Wanna play some darts?"

"That old game from Earth, huh? Do you still practice throwing knives? I don't want to be at a disadvantage."

"Not so much. I've never been as good as Jet."

A-Rail paused and looked at him a moment. Despite being wobbly, his stare was solid and certain. "You're the only one that never kept fighting after the boys folded shop. Why?"

For a second, Two Tone was speechless. These types of questions were not A-Rail's forte. "It was great when we were kids, man. But it wasn't going anywhere. I just grew up. Now I just want to be by myself. Is that so hard to get?"

Then Two Tone's old friend let something like a genuine smile pass his lips. That was a rarity.

"It's not hard to get at all," he responded.

A-Rail downed his beer and slammed the mug down. The old bartender grimaced. It was hard to blame him. The old man had been dealing with A-Rail all night, but he wouldn't do anything. There were few enough customers left in Cordova as it was, and he couldn't afford losing more. A-Rail was a wiry dude with crazy eyes, a scar over his left ear, and a smile that would bring any sensible man to question approach. Getting into it with him wasn't smart. Two Tone waved the old man away before his friend started something.

Thankfully there wasn't anyone in the place to cause a brawl. There hadn't been many people in the dive in ages, just as there wasn't many left in the city. Cordova had changed in a single way since they were kids. Everything decayed. Crime rose, jobs dried up, the gangs sprang up and people left one city in the Central for another. Cordova was no outlier—many cities were like it these days—but at least it wasn't Ganymede. Cordova was fortunate; it never became a hotbed of gangsters and crooked cops like that place. Instead of that, it rotted out. This crappy bar was much like the city itself. There was only the bouncer by the door, a middle-aged loner in a cheap leisure suit at a table, and one lush at the end of the bar. Back in the day you would never find a place like this empty. But times had changed; even A-Rail was different.

"You've been odd tonight," Two Tone said. "How many fights you gonna pick, and how many chicks you gonna squeeze later? Your beer goggles are on too tight."

"When did you get serious?"

"When I turned twenty-six." Two Tone downed his cool water glass hoping to distract his attention from the stench of sweat and recently cleaned vomit. Rapping his knuckles on the solid oak bar, he let his thoughts bleed out. "The Central is not as simple as we thought it was when we were kids. I mean, have you ever stopped to realize that we live in a giant prison? We're all in our little cells where we get plenty of bread and water, then we go to sleep, wake up, and do it again. Life isn't a rock n' roll song, A-Rail."

"That definitely doesn't sound like you."

"We haven't seen each other in seven years. Did you think I was still going to be that kid picking fights with other gangs to prove he's a tough cat? We only fought to keep our cells clean."

A-Rail fell silent for the first time that night.

"Come on, A-Rail. The Central is over two thousand miles long and filled with cities like Cordova separated by giant stone walls and metal gates. You can't fight steel. Sure we can go in and out, but they're still there. There's nowhere to go on this whole damn planet. You can't tell me that don't make you think."

"You just think too much." A-Rail called the bartender over. The old man produced a slim black slab, and A-Rail put his fingers on it. There was a pause before the register block made a ring, and the bartender smiled for the first time that night. The credits were paid. A-Rail waved him away. "Right, that's done."

Two Tone helped his friend off his stool. Now to get him home.

"I ain't got enough for an autotaxi," A-Rail mumbled. "You got enough, or do you still waste your pay dancing in those stupid rock clubs?"

"No, I killed a lot of old habits to get where I am. Haven't gone out on the town for years. The girls around here have terrible taste in music." Two Tone looked at his worn wristwatch. It was getting late. Neither of them bothered carrying phones. There was little service available in Cordova, and none in this area. "It's too expensive to get an autotaxi from here. Don't you have anyone we can call?"

"Don't you?"

"We'll just have to walk a few blocks to call one." Two Tone eyeballed his friend. "While we're at it, why did you call me out here?"

"I'll tell you when we're out of earshot of these hounds."

At the exit a hairless fat middle-aged man in a monkey suit sat beside a counter. He stood at Two Tone's approach and handed him a combat chain, and gave A-Rail a lead pipe. The two accepted their confiscated weapons and put on their jackets.

Two Tone knew how to use his chain. He was a bit rusty, but the rumors of people being attacked persisted. Certain folks had completely vanished. If there were gangs acting out there they'd soon regret running into two former members of the Jet Boys.

The small weights at the ends of the chain could crush bone with enough force, but most assailants didn't know that. Most hounds used knives and wouldn't see a chain coming. That advantage had cost certain stupid hounds some teeth. He slid the chain into his pocket, and left the bar.

Cracked concrete and soaked stone awaited them outside. There he saw the familiar weeds growing through the pavement and boarded up black brick buildings across the street. The smell of overcooked pasta and wet garbage blew into them. The wind was picking up. They ducked into an alley across the street as the rain cascaded out the rain gutters in heavy drops.

The cool breeze caused the hairs on Two Tone's neck to

stand up. He remembered the broken, empty buildings in this area.

"This was Ito Street Bomber territory."

"Until one of them got executed by the cops in broad daylight." A-Rail's grin flashed again. "That scared a lot of cats. Cordova used to be a hard place before that. Only the solid cats could stick around here. The cowards ran. Guess that's why the boys left. Do you still scare people, Two Tone?"

Two Tone ran a scarred hand across his soaked head, plastering down his naturally white hair which matched his skin. He had dyed it black when he was a kid to look tougher, but not these days. His flush cheeks and strong chin matched his dark brown—almost black—eyes, and his far too white skin gave him the appearance of a comic book zombie. That effect only doubled when he wore black clothes. He had his name for a reason.

"I'm not that guy anymore," Two Tone finally answered. He shook the water from his brown bomber jacket and wiped his casual blue jeans. "But I'm also not scared of the streets. Especially not with this."

Two Tone ran his fingers along his chain. Good weight. His fingertips instantly recalled memories of brawls long since won.

"You don't even need it." A-Rail rhythmically tapped the neighboring dumpster with his pipe as the pair passed. "Most of the hounds around here are either getting into cults or leaving this city for a better one with juicier targets. Even they know there's nothing left."

"You're also leaving."

"Yeah."

"This have anything to do with why you called me out here? It wasn't to reminisce about old times. You never get nostalgic. Tell me what's up."

"My dad used his connections to get me a job in Central 2106. Morningstar City. It's been a long time coming, but I'm getting out."

Two Tone slung the chain over his shoulders and shrugged. "This place is drying up. Makes sense."

A-Rail mindlessly nodded in agreement.

An arc of lightning split the cloud cover overhead. For an instant, Two Tone thought he saw the cascading shadows in the alley moving around him.

A pair of lean black cats bolted between trash cans into the dark. A-Rail laughed, but Two Tone sneered. His sixth sense was screaming like the thunder drumming above. A fight was coming.

"What was that thing that old man used to say?" A-Rail asked. "All cats are grey in the dark? No fooling. All those damn cats all look alike out here."

Two Tone wrapped a fistful of his chain in his right hand, stretched it out to its full length, and held the opposite end in his left with enough of a slack in the center.

A-Rail cocked a brow. "What are you doing?"

"We're being followed. I know it. Spend enough time in the quiet, and you learn to hear things."

"You learned to be paranoid. Get a woman, dreg."

The rain turned black as it slapped against their shoulders.

Two Tone looked up. Three shadows brandishing dark blades descended from the rooftops. He jumped back, and the alley pavement under him shattered into chunks, revealing tiny purple weeds clumping together. Three figures emerged from the rubble.

The first thing that Two Tone noticed was that he was wrong. They weren't shadows. They were deformed men with dark mud pouring out of every orifice. Their vacant soulless eyes let waterfalls of muck gush from the tear ducts of their sunken skulls. The musty air filled with the stink of corpses. These things were actual living monsters.

"The hell?!" A-Rail yelled.

The monsters fell upon the pair. A-Rail shouted as Two Tone moved in.

Two Tone flung the chain to the one in the center. The weapon struck down on its outstretched wrist, and the monster winced. The left one circled around to his back and sliced for his neck. He rolled forward, and rainwater ripped apart instead of his spine. Two Tone spun, and whipped the chain down. The weight struck the neck of the monster with a crack, sending it stumbling. Mud spilled onto the concrete at its crooked feet. Two Tone landed in a crouch between his two attackers.

The first mud man approached the tar puddle where the goo landed. The mud slid along the sidewalk into its foot, rejoining the body. Two Tone grimaced, and kept the ends of the chain held tight. The two enemies were on either side.

Then he noticed A-Rail was missing, as was the third aggressor.

"A-Rail?" he inquired. No answer. He swore to himself then to the two attackers. "I don't know what you dregs are supposed to be, but if you hurt A-Rail, I'm going to have to smash your bones to dust."

The pair sprang forward on each side of him. There was no room to dodge in the narrow alley.

Lightning flashed out of the corner of his eye. But it wasn't lightning. It was more like a golden snake gliding effortlessly through the tall dark grass of night. It slid beside him to the right. Two Tone followed. He dove to his right through trash cans, rolling through puddles in the process. The mud men crashed into each other.

Two Tone stood up, and ran forward into the street. That flash—he'd seen it before. He couldn't pinpoint where. Maybe a dream. Right now it didn't matter.

The monsters barrelled into the street behind him. He couldn't give them space. Two Tone bolted for the alley across the road. His shoulder scraped against the brick as he made it inside. He jumped forward, and kicked over a garbage can.

Wind whistled as they came in behind him.

One of the mud men howled as it slipped over the trash, blocking the second monster. The first one fell sideways. Static zipped through Two Tone and into his chain like an electromagnetic charge. A golden thread shone in the abyss of the falling monster's blackened mouth. It was his chance. He swung the chain to the open mouth.

The mud man ate the chain between its rows of black teeth. It struck the inside of the sunken skull. The head exploded, mud splashed against the alley like a mob hit. The lifeless corpse melted in the endless downpour into a puddle and evaporated into steam.

The second monster leaped over its ally for the prey.

Trash cans tumbled underfoot as Two Tone fell back. He grabbed hold of the bottom of a nearby dumpster to steady himself. But it was too late. The mud man fell upon him, knocking him to the drenched ground.

Blood sprayed as it slashed at his chest. The animal intensity is gave off was like nothing Two Tone had ever seen. He choked on screams as the monster grabbed at him.

Mud mittens from the beast wrapped around his throat. Sparks of pain shot through his skull and chest. His breaths choked, and his vision blurred as the mud fell across his eyes and down his throat. He pulled back on its deformed hands, but lacerations cut into his palms and fingers. Its body was sharp like jagged rocks under that mud. The monster's thick claw-like hands continued to cut into his throat.

This monster had a single-minded purpose: to kill. And it was succeeding. He uselessly clawed against it. The dark skies and storm faded into black.

Then he thought of A-Rail, and the dying world let a shape shoot into focus. The golden thread was not really golden at all. He could see its true translucence color slashing apart the grey dim of the dying city crumbling around his dead body and bringing it into focus. The ephemeral thread extended through his vision and twisted harmlessly out of the monster's head into the sky and exploded like a new star billions of miles away. It was like it was trying to keep him awake. For a moment, Two Tone died with the light.

But he couldn't afford to stay down. He pushed back against the monster's grip, his cuts fighting against him.

He waited for a spare breath, and then acted. His palm shot forward and struck the mud man's nose, sending whatever cartilage it had into its brain. The monster's head whirled in place, and then the creature fell over dead beside him.

As he panted, struggling to regain his composure, he kept an eye on the body. He didn't trust it. Monsters shouldn't even exist, so there was nothing to say it was actually dead. Two Tone flipped onto its back.

Something told him to keep attacking. It might have been dead, but it would be getting back up.

And it did.

The mud man bit and thrashed at him. Two Tone lined his chain across the monster's mouth, and wrapped it tight. He pressed his knee on its back and pulled back on the chain with all his might. It thrashed, and he held tight. He waited for the snap, but it never came.

Instead there was a hard whistle of escaping air, and the splash of mud hitting pavement like cymbal strike. The head had separated from the neck. The corpse melted in the rain.

"Choke on that, you bastard," he said.

Two Tone stumbled against the alley wall. His throat was raw, and his hands and chest stung. He let out a breath and touched his neck. Blood stained his fingers.

He took a step, and it hit him all once. Then he found himself kissing pavement. His legs had given out. Water flooded the world around him. He was done.

Above him stood a young man in a sharp black suit and short blond hair.

It would have almost been normal—if the suit wasn't carrying the severed black head of the missing third mud man. The suit smiled down at Two Tone like he was watching a caged animal.

"Sarpedon ain't gonna like this," the stranger said.

Then the silence swallowed the alleyway, and darkness followed.

Chapter 2
"The Dead City Cordova"

Intangible shapes formed in Two Tone's mind as he floated among the stars, pinpoints of light in the endless infinite. He drifted without rhyme or reason. The silence pierced the void around him before the relative whisper of a scream broke through. There was the dark blue planet, Achaea, spinning endlessly and alone in the barren universe.

He was in space, and he could breathe. Was he still alive?

Below him, the Central stretched as it did from coast to coast covering the entire Skia continent in the middle of the raging tall waves of the endless sea. The thousands of steel jungle cities were indistinguishable from each other especially from so high up. Pin pricks of light shone brighter in the dead cities like Cordova, Helice, the Steel Prairie, and Ganymede, and he found himself pulled toward them as if opposing magnets were built into the soil and his soul. That light from before was trying to tell him something.

There was no time to question it. Before he knew it, he was falling back down to the planet as if gravity had reached through space toward him. The planet drew closer, and heat burned into his bones. An electromagnetic charge snapped into him, sending spasms through his muscles. There he saw a vision of a pair of green eyes staring at him through the void. They saw everything he did, including his death.

Atmospheric pressure crushed him, and his flesh and bones incinerated. He became dust, at the same moment the electromagnetic charge left him. Like ball lightning, it shot off. There was nothing left of him.

But he was still alive.

His screams were non-existent, and yet he could hear them. The last thing he saw before he faded into the star shine of space were the two moons of Achaea watching him die. Those eyes of a long dormant demon laughing at the helpless rats below, just waiting for them to drown, had always kept watch over the remnants of those that landed so long ago. The shadow planet left nothing behind, and now it had devoured him.

Then he woke up.

The worst headache he'd had since his skull was slammed into a brick wall eleven years ago met him like an old friend. Bad drummers incessantly stomping a bass drum weren't half as annoying. He rolled over on his couch.

"Damn," he muttered, clutching his forehead.

He paused, opened his eyes, and sprang up. This was wrong. He was supposed to be in an alley. He was supposed to be dead.

But he wasn't. Two Tone was home, lying on his couch. There was no one else around.

The cracked grey drywall of the apartment quickly came into focus in the light of the old streetlamp outside. The dusty picture frames and the torn brown carpet were the same as ever. On the coffee table before him lay his chain and a glass of water he didn't remember pouring. His shoes and bomber jacket were lying in a pile by the door. How did he get back here?

He ran his fingers on his neck. There was a bandage around his throat where he had been cut. His fingers were also taped up as was his chest. Someone had patched him up.

Two Tone checked around. He double-checked the barren living room. The old kitchen was as empty as his fridge and cabinets, and the bathroom held nothing aside from his sink, toilet, and shower. His room was empty as usual except his mattress on the floor, his old record player and collection, and weights. The apartment was empty.

That creepy feeling of loneliness threatened to return. He shook it off. This was what he wanted. This was what he needed.

Wasn't it?

He fell back on the couch and groaned. None of this made sense, and he was still feeling raw. Not to mention that A-Rail was still out there. Then there was that man in the suit. He mentioned the name Sarpedon. What did that mean?

Then there were those mud men. When did monsters just decide to exist like that? He hardly believed it himself. Did those things have to do with the missing people?

The phone rang, and he nearly jumped out of his skin. The clock told him it was half past one. No one should be calling him now.

His telephone was the old rotary style made for collectors of ancient Earth trinkets. Since he didn't bother with a cell phone, due to poor service, this was the only way to go. It comes with the territory of having archaic taste, but it worked against him. He had no way of knowing who was calling.

Maybe it was A-Rail.

"Hello," Two Tone said.

"Mr. Fisher," a woman responded. Her voice lacked any sense of emotion.

"It's Two Tone. Who is this?"

"You can call me *Green Eyes*."

Just like the dream. "Right, lady. What do you want?"

"It's what *you* want. You want your friend, correct?"

He waited.

"Good," she said. "Now drink the water on the coffee table."

"So you put this here. What's in it?"

"I didn't put it there, but I know who did. We don't have time for this. Listen to me, Two Tone; if you want to live, you need to drink it."

"It's just water."

"It is, but to explain more would only confuse you right now. Don't worry, if I wanted to kill you, I wouldn't wait for you to wake up to do it."

He lifted the glass and inspected it. It was just ordinary

tap water. He would have just ignored her, but his voice was gripped by parchedness, and his body felt somewhat heavy. Dizziness overtook him.

Two Tone downed the drink. The cool sensation shocked him awake.

"Good," Green Eyes said. Her tone remained emotionless. "Now as to your friend . . ."

"This have anything to do with that hound in the suit?"

"That's getting rather far ahead of yourself, Two Tone. For now, you must head to the harbor. There is someone at Warehouse Sixteen you will want to meet."

"Are you trying to blackmail me into a hit, lady? I don't do that. My chain is for keeping the dirty hounds off my back and away from my stuff. If this whole thing was a mob scouting, I'm gonna be plenty pissed."

It was tiring. No matter how many times the gangs crushed the mob they still kept coming back like the rain season, and rain was as common as getting jumping used to be. Of course the mobs mainly died off with the gangs, but that didn't stop an ambitious punk from starting up again every now and then. Cordova was a glorified roach motel.

"I understand your paranoia," she said, "but it's misguided. Go to the harbor, and you will understand what it is you are dealing with."

"I don't get any of this," Two Tone said. "What's your game?"

"You will find what you need at the warehouse. I'm certain you have been there before."

"Yeah, I have. I spilled some blood there a long time ago."

"Then go. Good luck, Two Tone. If it be allowed, we will speak again."

The phone clicked.

He sat back on the couch. This could be a trap—but for what reason? The old gangs were all gone now. Either they had been disbanded, fled to other cities, or had gotten too big for their britches and began attacking cops. The executions in the streets some of these lowlifes received even churned Two Tone's stomach, but it wasn't unexpected. Cordova was nothing but cracked ceilings and shattered windows now. What could he find in this city?

This woman was a fool. What would be worth finding in this endless wasteland of broken bottles and discarded needles? If she wanted his help, she was wasting her time.

But he would still go.

A-Rail needed him. The last thing he would ever do would be to leave a friend behind. Cats in Cordova recognize honor, or at least they used to. There was no chance Two Tone would forget that.

He changed into new clothes, discarding his torn rags. He chose a grey hoodie and black pants. No sense in attracting attention so late at night.

The gashes on his neck were still raw under his bandages, just as his fingers still vaguely throbbed. The chest wound had bruised purple, but there was no blood. No one would think him out of the ordinary if they saw him out there. He finished changing and made his way to the front door.

There was a handwritten note posted that said, "*Drink the water.*"

21

Two Tone crumpled it and threw it to the floor. His last nerve was flaring. Whoever brought him back couldn't even be bothered to leave a name. Damn hounds.

He stepped outside the apartment and closed the door. Cracked drywall and dusty carpets filled the hall. He put his hand on the tiny scanner beside the door. The pad recognized his handprint, and the door locked. Of course that wouldn't matter if the power went out, but there was no sense not trying.

Light shone from an open doorway across the hall. An old woman with wrinkles more plentiful than leeches in a swamp glowered at him. She wore an old ratty nightgown and hair cap that matched her personality. Nothing worse than neighbors who are incapable of minding their business. The granny pointed a hooked finger at him.

"You look like you fell down some stairs," she said. "Where are you going so late looking like that? Kids have no sense these days."

Two Tone sighed. "How many times do I have to tell you to close the damn door? You don't know who might get into the building."

"No respect for the elderly, huh? Rotten boy."

"Just shut the door and go to bed!"

The walls shook as she complied.

On the way down to the street, he thought about how he would get to the harbor. Autotaxis were half-price between one and four in the morning, and there was less of a chance at being spotted so late. Not to mention that most hounds stayed away from them due to all the cameras they had. It was the most obvious choice of getting there in one piece. Shame he'd have to cut into his savings, but there was no getting around that.

Lit streetlamps and locked buildings waited with a lightened drizzle outside the foyer. It was dead silent. Cordova slept like a corpse.

There were three panels by the front entrance. The first was the black pad like the one on every apartment door. The second was a red panel for emergencies. The third was his target. He placed his hand on the white panel, and a small hum rumbled, before a ring broke the silence. His print was scanned, and the call was made.

Within seconds a medium-sized yellow and white striped car sped down the rain-soaked street. It slammed to a stop right in front of the steps with an irksome precision. It was difficult trusting something so immaculate.

He laid a hand on the cold panel beside the rear door; it beeped, hummed, and then swung open. The car closed behind him like a refrigerator door. The stink of turpentine enclosed on him as he sat on the stiff cushions.

"*Good evening*," a toneless pre-recorded female voice said through the speaker. "*I hope you are well.*"

"Yeah, sure," he replied.

The autotaxi was split in two. A large thick glass wall lay between the front area and passengers in the back. Two Tone's seat was soft enough, but it was difficult to get comfortable when he knew what was under it. Any attempt to cause a disturbance, pull up the seat, or be a general nuisance, would unleash the electric volts stored in the battery inside. They were no different from police cars in that respect. Punks have a hard time messing with autotaxis because they're so dangerous.

And it wasn't as if there was a reason to mess with them. There was no actual driver like in the old movies—instead a thick metal pole that stretched from the ceiling down through the seat and into the floor was in their place. It was a 360 degree camera that scanned both the road ahead and the passenger seats for disturbances. There was another similar pole on the passenger side.

They were designed after old cars like the ones Two Tone saw on his ancient album covers. But no one drove anymore. No reason to when the autotaxis are cheaper and take you anywhere.

"*Where would you like to go?*" the inhuman voice inquired.

Two Tone thought for a second. The cops could get the records if they wanted to. "Castelo Boulevard."

There was a click and hum followed by a pause. An irritating beep followed.

"*Destination selected. Please enjoy your trip!*"

He grimaced. There were over five thousand cities in the Central, and as far as he knew, they all were run by these autotaxis. Different companies, of course, but it was the same general idea. How could anyone stand it? The voice sounded so real and yet *off* at the same time. It was impossible to trust anything that's incapable of acknowledging your existence.

"Just drive. Ain't nothing I hate more than machines that talk back."

Finally the car moved. Two Tone stretched back in his seat, his hands behind his sore neck.

"*Please keep your feet on the floor and your hands off the separation glass. Thank you once more for choosing Grand Getaway's Autotaxi Service. We very much appreciate your patronage.*"

"I get it already. You guys watchin' from the cameras must get awful sick of hearing that all the time. I know I am. Your job's worse than mine."

The ride was as boring as expected. A long time ago, around the time he was a boy, they used to have more options for passengers. The speakers would allow for direct communication with those in customer service; that was how it worked until complaints of harassment shut them up. Customers also had options for music until similar objections grounded that approach. This made travel as exciting as watching cement harden.

The empty, broken streets reminded him of the old days. Not the days of his youth, but the days long ago before Cordova became what it did. Because it rains so much on Achaea, food grows easily, and the animals brought by the original colonists mated more than any rational being would prefer to think about it. Over five hundred years ago when the original Leader created the Central, he created specialized farm areas in each of the thousands of cities. Vertical farming warehouses allowed for more controlled production and steady jobs for those who wanted them, but since every city had them it made little difference when Cordova succumbed to itself. The rise of the black market, attempts at prohibition, and general malaise due to high comfort levels, slowly twisted this place over the centuries. Half a century after landing on Achaea, and they were sliding into barbarism.

But right now none of that mattered. He tried to remember the face of that guy in the suit. The punk looked out of his element, like a boy trying to wear his dad's clothes. Then there was that smile. Whoever this Sarpedon was he must be—

Two Tone's throat seized, and breaths choked out of him. He gripped hard on his neck.

"Please keep your feet on the floor and your hands off the separation glass."

He thrashed and elbowed the window as his eyes bulged. Black liquid trickled from his lips with struggled breaths. He clawed at the cut skin on his neck. Something was inside and strangling him.

"If you require medical aid, please pull the tab at the base of the glass."

Then he bent over the seat and wheezed. Fist-sized globs slowly slid from his mouth like tar. He coughed violently and shook his head. The tar clung to his throat, refusing to let go. But still he coughed and swung his neck until the substance broke free and splashed against the seat splashing like vomit. Air flooded back into his lungs.

He fell back into his seat, struggling to regain his composure. Sweat poured down his cheeks.

"If you require medical aid—"

"Shut up already!" He kicked the glass.

"*Warning*," the voice replied. "*You will be forcefully ejected if this disturbance continues.*"

"Got it, Mom. Now piss off."

The voice fell silent, but Two Tone's irritation did not fade. The small mass of black liquid pooled on the seat, stinking of rotting flesh and bone. He ran a finger through it to find it was much thicker than vomit or phlegm should be.

Almost like mud.

Two Tone felt for the chain in his pocket. Whatever he was dealing with was far more complicated than a shaggy looking kid in a suit. And A-Rail was wrapped up in this whole thing.

"*Bile detected*," the voice finally said. "*You will be charged extra for cleaning services. We hope you understand.*"

He leaned against the window and stared out into the dead of night. This thing was moving much too slow.

"I understand."

Chapter 3
"The Man with the Moving Skin"

Two Tone ditched the autotaxi on Castelo Boulevard and walked the rest of the way to the harbor. Tall steel buildings loomed like giants over the vacant streets. During the day there would be autotaxis and pedestrians to fill the empty spaces but night was a whole different world. Tonight, there was nothing and no one but him.

The harbor lay down the road. He advanced through old rusted gates, keeping to the shadows of the giant cargo boxes and abandoned cranes and carriers. There were few functional lights along the main path; he kept to the dark. The southbound road led along the water's edge.

There hadn't been gang activity here since the Ice Devils were destroyed. That scared a lot of people at the time. Those creeps held up in the mostly unused Warehouse Sixteen, and it was very hard to get the drop on them. They simply knew every place in the harbor: every port, and every shortcut, better than anyone else. Then they got stupid.

Eventually they began attacking cops by jumping and

shooting them with their own guns.

There was an unwritten rule in Cordova to never use firearms due to the DNA trigger that is required to shoot. It scans and replicates the DNA on the bullet making every shot easy to trace. On top of it, if anyone is caught without that trigger, they could be executed by police without trial. No law is really enforced in Cordova except involving firearms. This also makes avoiding cops really easy—unless you get cocky.

Everyone knows the cops have sonic scanners. They track gunshots through the supersonic sound of the shot as well as the explosion of gunpowder, the sound pressure level, and resultant gas from the barrel to pinpoint the shot's location. These convoluted devices were installed in all the radars in police stations in Cordova and many other cities. Using a firearm is suicide.

If the Ice Devils had brains they would still be alive to terrorize dregs like Two Tone and the Jet Boys. But they're all gone now.

Two Tone kept his hood low over his eyes, and looked out over Cordova Bay. There were no ships out, and there probably wouldn't be until next week, but the bay had a large gate on the opposite side of the water to correspond with the wall to Ganymede, the next Central city. It was used for trade between the two cities, but it mainly served as a border these days. Given the history of both Cordova as a gang ridden hellhole and Ganymede as mobster central, it was a border most strayed from. That was why the Jet Boys loved to come here.

Small rock formations of granite lay beside the bay. Two Tone crossed a jetty over shallow waters as the drizzle sprayed from the cloud cover above. Warehouse Sixteen was just ahead.

He crossed an alley and leaned against the neighboring warehouse. He made sure to keep outside the light. Old trash cans and dumpsters sat strewn about around him in the dark.

Whispers mumbled from behind one of the damp receptacles. No matter where he glanced, the source could not be found.

"Hey!" the voice repeated. It was from behind the dumpster ahead.

He barely made out the figure, but the face was easily enough to place. It was a woman wearing a heavy hood.

"You talking to me?" he asked.

"Who else would I be talking to? Come over here!"

The woman sat in a pile of rags between dumpsters. The small figure wore a torn up old coat, dirty stockings and shoes, and a hood covering her head. She was a mess. He couldn't make out anything about her under her old clothes, but he couldn't imagine her looking better than this. He approached her slowly.

"What do you want, girl?" Two Tone asked.

"I don't want anything from you," she replied, still whispering. "I'm warning you to stay away from that warehouse. There's trouble in there."

He nodded to himself. It wasn't the same woman who called him earlier. The voice on the phone was cold, emotionless. This voice was different—soft like a gentle breeze. "What's your name?"

"Aurora," she softly stated. "Does it matter?"

"Names matter. How else would I know what to call you? So, Aurora, are you with the blond guy in the suit? Is he here?"

"Blond guy? There is no blond guy here. There's a monster in that warehouse. I'm waiting for him."

Two Tone raised a brow. "This monster wouldn't happen to have mud covering them, would they?"

The rain overtook her voice, so he asked her to repeat herself. The weather could be unpredictable. The drizzle thickened momentarily then thinned out once more.

"There is a man called Sarpedon in there," she said. "You cannot just charge in inside."

There was that name again. "Maybe I should."

"Then he will kill you."

"I have every reason to believe my friend is in there, girl. I'm not abandoning him. I ain't no hound."

"Do you think your friend wants you dead? How about your family? You'll never see them ever again."

"They're all gone." He leaned around the dumpster to see her face, but the girl backed further behind it. Her illusiveness was starting to annoy. "But I'm still here. So I'm going inside."

"Stop!"

Two Tone dashed from the alley across the road. He ducked around the streetlight beams.

The warehouse glass was as cracked and broken as the

rest of Cordova. Old boards blocked every window and doorway. He carefully circled around the building. On the north side he spotted a loose board. He pried it open and sidled through the opening. The musty lukewarm air punched him in the face and the taste of stale beer twisted his tongue.

Broken boards and drenched dust littered the small hall before him. He stepped slowly and lightly. Packs of rats scurried to and fro. A voice bounced against the walls from deeper inside.

"They're both late," a woman said. "I don't like it."

Two Tone slid around the corner. It was the warehouse interior. Tall catwalk scaffoldings swirled above him and old rotting crates were peppered about the large open space. Three well-dressed figures stood in the center, all looking like they were headed to the hop downtown. There was a large gate to the outside on the opposite side of the warehouse from Two Tone that the trio were watching. He crouched low and inched closer as they continued their business.

"We don't need anyone but us," the man with a cowboy hat murmured.

"We need everyone, Graves!" she shouted back.

The man with his back to Two Tone grunted. "Would you two stop talking?"

Silence fell. Standing in the penumbra made it hard to grasp the form of the tall man except as a broad shouldered shadow in a dark suit. It wasn't the man Two Tone saw before he went under earlier, but there was a vibe about this hound. Two Tone knew tough hounds when he spotted them. This man was no stooge—he was dangerous.

Two Tone waited. It was a good five minutes before anyone spoke again.

"They're here," the woman said.

Graves chuckled. "Always with the obvious, Lorna."

The gate to the outside finally swung open. Streetlamp lights reflecting off the downpour brightened the cavernous space. A burly man wearing a grey suit and holding an umbrella stepped inside. He slid the gate shut behind him.

The woman huffed. "Where have you been, Turk?"

"Searching for Templeton," he said. "He gave me the slip. Another man's dead. Erich lost his head."

Graves laughed lightly. "Two of you couldn't take down one punk?"

"Shut your mouth, Graves," Turk barked out.

"You were supposed to watch him." Graves tipped the brim of his hat further over his eyes. "How many times do you get to screw up, while we pull your slack? While you were messing around, we got the Sarpedon's target over in Warehouse Three."

"It isn't like you were any better at catching that traitor."

"Enough," the tall man said. "Lazlo and the others can take care of *that*. We have much more important business to discuss. That being, should we stay in Cordova or move to greener pastures. The legends of this place have been disappointing. It was not worth coming up from the dirt for this slaughter. There isn't anything worth saving in Cordova."

"Sarpedon," Turk said to the tall man, "I don't see why we're here in the first place."

Two Tone's eyes widened. This was the guy that kid mentioned! Was this monster looking for that punk Two Tone saw in the alley before he lost consciousness? They weren't friends? This didn't make any sense.

"It's no wonder that you don't see why we're here," Sarpedon asked. He placed a shadowy hand on Turk's shoulder, and slid it up his thick neck. "That's because you don't see anything."

With a twist, Sarpedon ripped the face off of Turk. The blanket of skin liquefied in mid-air and struck the ground in a splash. But there was no blood, no flesh. No longer was there a leathery-skinned man staring back at Sarpedon, but a smooth black shape as if his features had been ironed off and painted over. Turk slumped into the waiting embrace of Sarpedon.

The faceless man muffled a scream. His arms and legs thrashed about.

"You had enough time out," Sarpedon whispered. "Have some rest, Turk. You've earned it."

Turk twisted and flailed, but he couldn't escape the iron grip of Sarpedon. The tall man pulled, and Turk's body sunk into Sarpedon like he was quicksand. The burly man's fate was sealed. Within a second, he was gone, as were the screams. He'd sunken into Sarpedon's body and vanished without a trace.

At that moment, Two Tone was able to finally focus on the others. They were both the same as Turk; murky shadow figures disguised by clothes and fake skin fashioned by something like mud. He bit his lip and kept quiet. What the hell was going on in Cordova?

"Now that we've settled that," Sarpedon simply stated, "how goes our progress?"

A hand landed on Two Tone's shoulder. Hairs on his neck stiffened. Slowly he turned his head. Behind him stood a figure in a long and heavy brown hood and jacket. The cloaked figure gestured back to the exit. It was the girl from before, she followed him.

Two Tone quietly tailed her back out. She kept silent the whole way.

The rain was lightening a bit when he got outside. He leaned the board back against the door as she went ahead. The girl led him to the alley across the way from before.

The shorter figure in the hood kept her back to him. She was shivering. Whether it was the cold or something else he couldn't tell.

"Aurora?" he asked.

"Yes?"

"What were those things?"

"I told you to stay out."

"That's why I went. I still have places to go." He grabbed her by the shoulder. "Tell me."

She pulled back. "Why do you need to know?"

"I have a friend in trouble. Who was that Sarpedon thing? Does he have anything to do with those attacks around Cordova?"

Finally she pried loose from him. "Sarpedon is a

murderer. He's killed many without thinking twice, and I'm going to be the one to kill him."

"I don't think a woman should be forced to do a man's job." He looked back out the alley once more. No one had followed them. "They said something about Warehouse Three. I'm going to see what that's about."

"Do you think I'm warning you because I find this fun? Stay out of this, or you really will die."

"Been there."

"What?"

She wasn't being nasty about it, but this girl was out of her element. She was shaking and completely unable to look him in the eye. Only Two Tone could deal with this mess.

"Get going," Two Tone said. "I'll take care of it."

He left her behind, following the warehouse numbers through the harbor.

There were too many uncertainties. He'd barely survived a fight with two of those mud things, and there were three more of them back there. When he was younger Two Tone was well known for skinning tough cats. But those were humans, and surviving fights was easy when he planned ahead. Running into a den of unknowns was a good way to get killed.

Warehouse Three looked exactly the same as the other abandoned buildings did, but there was a clear difference. From his position in the alley he saw a low light shining out of the cracked windows. Someone was nearby.

He took a breath and fingered the chain in his right pocket. This time he probably wouldn't get away unscathed.

These hounds weren't the same as the mindless monsters he fought earlier—these ones had brains. He needed to survey the area and make a plan.

"You didn't have to follow me," he said over his shoulder.

Aurora stood behind him, rainwater falling from her ratty hood. She had followed from a close enough distance. "You'll have better odds with someone to help."

"I'll have better odds if you tell me what I'm up against."

"You brought up mud men before."

"I did."

Her mouth fell open. "Where did you see them?"

"Fought them a few hours ago. Took one of their heads off at the jaw."

"You look remarkably calm."

"I've never seen a monster before, and I admit this is crazy. I barely believe what's going on, but it's been an odd night. Just tell me what they are, so I can kill them easier."

She took a deep breath. "It's hard to say. Sarpedon is . . . not human. At least, I don't think so. He took over Ganymede months ago from out of nowhere. The mob world was overturned. He's trying to create some kind of kingdom on Achaea. Whatever he is, he's dealing with dark forces."

"Thanks." He waved her back. "Wait here."

Then a grunt caught his attention. He rounded the old building, advancing slowly. He paused, reached for his chain, and then sidled up to the warehouse wall. The grunt repeated, more muffled this time. It wasn't in the building, but behind it. He soon reached the rear.

Two Tone peered around the corner, and his stomach churned. There were three men in suits standing in a circle and holding umbrellas. In the middle of them was a large brown sack that was bulging and thrashing. Someone was inside.

That someone had to be A-Rail.

The three all had the same slick suit, streaked with mud like sweat, wearing different colored wide brim hats and dark trench coats. Their lips were thin, their cheeks slightly bulging, and all were well-built. The three took turns kicking the sack as if it were a puppy needing a newspaper to the nose.

"Is it time, Lazlo?" the one closest to the warehouse asked.

The one beside him shook his head. "No."

"I'm taking a smoke break," the last said. "This is taking too long."

"You just had one, Smith."

Smith laughed. "You have no concept of time, Jenkins. If phone service doesn't work, you could always wear a watch instead. No tracking that way. Plan ahead. If Sarpedon had planned ahead, I would already be out of this damn rain."

"Well," Jenkins began, "Sarpedon said to wait until the meeting was over before we dump the trash. What he says goes. Come on, Lazlo, back me up."

Lazlo remained silent.

Smith laughed. "If I knew we were going to wait to kill street trash, I would have brought more cigs. Why do we need to wait for them to finish anyway? He's a waste of skin cells. Once he's underwater, we can finally get on with it. What's the point waiting?"

"Yeah, but still . . ." Jenkins tipped his brown hat. "We should wait. Sarpedon says."

Lazlo groaned and stepped away from the pair. He wandered toward the dock and stared out toward the large gate to Ganymede miles off.

Jenkins blinked, and then turned to Smith. "Was it something I said?"

"Whatever," Smith replied. He kicked the bag once more.

Two Tone paid the trio very little mind. He kept his right hand tapping against his chain, and his stare transfixed on the sack. Cordova might be falling apart with monsters crawling all over the place, but the least punks could do was stick together. Jet Boys don't run.

His neck wounds flared. He sniffed the air; the stink of rotting flesh wafted through the rain soaked docks. The smell of mud men arrived with the hardening rain.

There were three monsters before him, and those things in the warehouse would be on their way soon. Time to think fast. He held his chain tight.

"A-Rail," Two Tone muttered. "I'm on my way."

Chapter 4
"Shot Across the Harbor"

Smith crossed back around to the front of the building and Two Tone followed from the shadows. Crates and rusting dumpsters were strewn about everywhere—even in the alleys. The suit leaned against the warehouse corner with his umbrella propped against it. The rain poured off the ledge above him, leaving him relatively dry. He drew a cigarette and lit it.

From behind a dumpster, Two Tone leaned and watched. He kept his distance and waited for an opening.

"This is a waste of time," Smith said between puffs. "When did I fall so low on the ladder that I have to babysit a meatsack? Should just kill those two and say he got away. At least then I'd be doing something productive. I'm never going back in there . . ."

This was Two Tone's only chance. Sarpedon and his idiots would be on their way soon, and he still had the other two to worry about. He felt for the chain in his pocket.

Across the alleyway a figure emerged across the road. He

made a double take to confirm it was actually Aurora.

She stopped in the middle of a large puddle; her black boots soaked, she gestured at Smith. He squinted at the girl's arrival.

"Well, hey," Smith said. He flicked his cigarette away. "Some action."

Aurora pulled back her hood. Long auburn hair tumbled loose over her shoulders. Her high cheekbones, and ocean blue eyes like cold ice, clashed against the filth of the harbor around her. Whoever she was, she clearly didn't belong here. Two Tone found himself staring. Aurora was a whole other woman underneath the dirt.

"What are you doing out here, bitch?" Smith asked. He crossed the road toward her, without his umbrella. He tipped his hat and rainwater rolled off the side. "Do you know where you are?"

"Have you seen my daddy?" She asked in a childish pitch. "He's a big man in a grey suit. Mommy's waiting for him to come home. Is he here?"

Smith stopped just before the puddle before her. He grimaced.

"A dirty vagrant, huh? Being retarded is gonna cost you."

Smith went for his belt. A knife slipped loose from behind his back. "But fun is fun."

She took a step back. Her red lips tightened as she glanced past her attacker into the dark. Was she looking at Two Tone?

Smith paused for a moment then took one step into the puddle after her.

The full weight of Two Tone's charge knocked Smith off his feet. The smoker landed face first in the puddle before Aurora. Pooled water splashed out in large waves. Smith's screams muffled as he thrashed. The knife flew free and splashed into the puddle. Two Tone sat on his back and held him down.

From his pocket, Two Tone drew his chain. He whipped it around Smith's mouth and pulled back. He would do the same thing he did back in that alley to kill that monster. Smith's hat fell from his head.

Pops and clicks cracked from the thug, but the head did not give way. Instead, it turned around like a screw—and faced Two Tone. The muddied jaw face melting in the rain gaped at him, streaks of skin melting from his dented face. Eyes and mouth were sliding free as if from a soaked art canvas.

Smith's limbs and bones bucked and twisted. He wasn't a mud man like in the alley; this thing was another kind of beast.

Two Tone tossed his chain aside. He grabbed the brown slicked skull and slammed it down. Puddle water splashed everywhere. Black steam rushed out of Smith's cut head. Bones twisted as the force of the monster flailed against his weight.

"Here!" Aurora said.

She tossed Smith's fallen knife, and Two Tone caught it. It was a few inches long like a hunting knife, but there was a strange pattern engraved on the side like old characters from a language long dead. There was something foreign about it. Two Tone had never seen a blade like it before.

He slashed the knife across Smith's backwards neck, and black tar blood gushed out and into the puddle. Two Tone shoved the head into the puddle, and one last muffled scream escaped through the water. Bubbles flooded out as the monster was held down.

The thrashing ceased, and Smith went limp. Two Tone dunked into the puddle as if sliding through wet sand. The dark remains of Smith bobbed across the water in mud clumps. The remains steamed out into the storm, and eventually vanished.

Two Tone climbed out of the water and grunted. So they did have similarities with the mud monsters. They died the same way. "Haven't lost my touch."

"You dropped this." Aurora handed him his chain.

"Thanks," he said, pocketing it again. "That was a stupid risk baiting him like you did."

"I know. That was different for me. I guess I just . . . forget it. How did you get over here so fast? I barely saw you move when he pulled that knife."

"I was a dancer when I was younger. Not the kind you think. Mostly in Rock clubs to the beat. To be a dancer, you need to know how to move without wasting energy, and to a steady rhythm. Everybody has a rhythm—you just have to feel it out." He took a last sideways glance at the puddle where the monster evaporated. "Apparently, even monsters have one."

She watched him carefully. "Who are you? I've never seen anyone like you around here."

"Name's Two Tone. Like I told you: I'm here because these hounds took my friend." He turned back toward the warehouse. "And now to get him."

"Wait, you can't take on two of them alone. Call some of your friends or something. You're in a gang right? You look it."

"*Was*. And how did you figure out I ran with a gang?"

"Cordova is known for street toughs, and you fight like it. I thought there would be more like you here, but I haven't seen any since I got here."

He reached for Smith's abandoned umbrella and tossed it back to Aurora.

"Wait here this time," Two Tone said. "Fighting isn't for women."

"Do you have to go it alone?"

He glanced over his shoulder as he left. "Do you? At least I know I can handle myself."

Two Tone passed the warehouse once more. When he reached the dock, both of Smith's pals were still where he left them. Lazlo was on the dock, and Jenkins was harassing the prisoner in the bag. They were at least thirty feet apart with their umbrellas raised and not moving from their locations. Two Tone hid behind a crate and shimmied closer to A-Rail.

Jenkins looked over his shoulder toward the warehouse. "Are you sure you didn't hear anything, Lazlo?"

"No," he replied, unmoving. He was staring across the water at Ganymede. "For the last time, there's nothing out there. Smith probably found a rat to drown. He is an artist at killing."

Jenkins took hold of the bag and strode toward the water. He glanced nervously over his shoulder back toward the warehouse, his cheeks sweating brown streaks. The bag thrashed.

He was going to throw A-Rail in!

Two Tone ran from his cover into the rain. Jenkins looked up, but it was too late. Two Tone rammed him in the back, sticking Smith's knife in the monster's spine. Jenkins howled, and tumbled forward. He spun downward into the bay.

Two Tone took the bag. Jenkins heavy splash sounded a moment later.

Lazlo turned back, alerted by the noise.

Steam gushed out of the bay where the monster fell. Jenkins flailed and screamed as the water swallowed him. Lazlo blandly watched his ally die.

"Smith won't be rejoining you," Two Tone said. He rounded the dock toward Lazlo. "I don't think that cat can swim either."

Lazlo drew a knife that looked a lot like Smith's. He pointed it at Two Tone. "You shouldn't have come here."

Two Tone flashed a wolfish grin. "The last big shot who said that to me walks with a cane and drinks from a straw. You might not remember the Jet Boys, but everyone else that crossed us does. Either piss off, or come at me. You won't like where the second option gets you."

"Do you even know who we are?" Lazlo tossed his umbrella aside. "I am far more gracious than my compatriots. If you beg for forgiveness, you will be granted a slow death instead of what you deserve. I find that more than fair for devils."

Two Tone moved in and drew his chain. Lazlo sidestepped easily as the weapon struck air. Two Tone swore: the puddle water had soaked his clothes and slowed him down. Lazlo's knife slashed across the ex-thug's chest, and his elbow slammed against Two Tone's right eye.

Two Tone fell to a knee, and shook his head. Behind him, Lazlo moved in, readying his knife. Two Tone wasn't fast enough to take him—not like this. The blade plunged for his back.

An explosion ran out across the harbor, and wind whipped across the dock. Lazlo reeled. A bullet had struck his chest and mud burst out the wound like a grenade blast.

Off in the distance, a high pitched alarm screeched on. It was from the police station six blocks away. The scanner was echoing over the harbor. But there was no time for that.

Two Tone leaped up and slammed his chain against Lazlo's right temple with all his might. Lazlo swung back, but the knife was caught in the chain. Two Tone pulled the attacker in close. He wrapped Lazlo's arm, stepped forward and twisted, flipping Lazlo over his shoulder. The monster tumbled across his back and down into the water below. Like Jenkins, he bellowed as the bay ate at his flesh.

Within seconds he disappeared under the waves, and steam plumed from the water. He did not resurface.

Behind Two Tone, Aurora was shivering and pointing a handgun where Lazlo had just been standing. She was frozen solid. Meanwhile, the alarm continued blaring, and sirens were beginning to sound. They had to leave immediately.

"Hey," Two Tone called out to the girl. She didn't respond. "Hey!"

Finally she looked at him, her hands shaking violently with the rest of her.

"Help me open the bag!" he said. "The cops will be here soon."

The girl flinched and put her firearm in her coat. She ran over and helped him tear open the bag.

Sirens screamed into the night. There wasn't a lot of time. The cops barely enforced any laws in Cordova, but this was the big one—the unspoken taboo. Aurora would be killed for this.

When the pair finally opened the bag, Two Tone's heart sank. It wasn't A-Rail. It wasn't even a friend. It was far worse.

The slightly out of shape middle-aged man with black hair and a greasy smile to match stared at his saviours. He wasn't very tall, but he cut an imposing figure. His pinstripe suit was dirty and torn, but his hard-worn leathery face was the same as ever. He laughed in surprise when he saw Two Tone.

"Two Tone?" Stagger Lee said. "You actually saved my life."

"Not now, Stagger. We need an exit. Cops are coming. Do you have a shelter nearby?"

He blinked, and glanced around the harbor. "Yes. A few streets north of here."

The three escapees hurried from the dock. They cut

across road where Smith had drowned, Two Tone leading. Flashing lights cut into the overcast sky and into the harbor gates. Police cars turned out into the down the empty roads back where Two Tone had entered from. The three runners blazed forward, cutting through the same alley Two Tone had first met Aurora.

Sirens buzzed everywhere. They passed the first block of warehouses and then the second. Strangely, there were no cop cars streaming down the alleyways toward them.

But that wouldn't last long.

After the following block was the fence before the street. Cargo crates and empty containers lay strewn to their right and left, giving much shelter. Behind them the red and blue sirens cut through the harbor. Voices muffled in the alleys between the warehouses. Cops were getting closer.

They reached the fence and Two Tone looked out into the street ahead. There was no gate nearby—and it was certainly guarded by now. He asked Stagger for their destination.

There was a short pause. "The Reyes Quality Convenience Mart. Do you know where that is?"

"Yes, just two streets over. Can you climb?" He watched the chubby man scurry over, and then Two Tone turned back to Aurora. "Hey, girl. Hey! Wake up."

She blinked and came to life once more. "I hear you, Two Tone."

He took her by the shoulders and stared her down. She looked up at him, puzzled. Her red lips crinkled in a thin frown. "Wake up. You heard the man. We need to go over the fence."

"But I—"

"Not now. I know you didn't want to kill him, but we can't do this now. If the cops get you, you're dead. You wanna live to get Sarpedon? Then get over the fence."

"Why are you helping me?"

"We'll figure that out later. Now climb!"

The two scrambled over the metal fence. Two Tone glanced back to spot blaring flashlights shining from the alley and highlighting the darkness around the crates. Megaphone voices screeched into the night petitioning surrender. They were getting close.

Two Tone and his compatriots sprinted up the empty street. He kept thinking about Aurora and what happened to the Ice Devils. Sure there were no bodies, and therefore no real evidence, but this was not a crime you debated in Cordova. This girl wouldn't live to see her revenge at this rate. He might not even live to see the morning.

The convenience store was just ahead. A half-lit neon sign told their location and allowed them to run around the back. There they finally took a breather.

Stagger struggled for air, and Aurora held her chest, but Two Tone kept watching the barren streets. Soon the cops would start knocking on doors for witnesses and suspects.

Aurora leaned against the old brick on opposite side of the alley from him. After a beat her composure started to return. She had finally regained some color and her breath.

"Your friend," she said. "You found him! I can't believe it. When you said he was involved with Sarpedon, I really thought he was dead."

"My friend?" Two Tone looked at her sideways. "Stagger is not my friend. He's a backstabber."

Stagger Lee ran his fingers through his unkempt hair and let out a sigh. "Come on, Two Tone. Don't be that way."

"Stagger," Two Tone said with disgust. "I was looking for A-Rail. Not you."

The girl blinked. "Stagger?"

"I can tell you're not from around here. He's just a club owner and a real hound. But why monsters like Sarpedon are after him is a question I want answered."

Stagger scratched at the stubble on his chin and flashed a toothy grin. "Why indeed?"

"Do you know where A-Rail is?" Two Tone asked. "No games."

"Let us find a better place to talk. Last thing we want is for the cops to catch us shooting the breeze out in the cold."

Stagger lead them up nearby stairs behind the store. He used a very odd combination of knocks, and the door swung open. Two Tone and Aurora followed him in.

They stepped into a back room covered in old black paint where a group of shady men wearing fancy shirts and far too much hair product sat playing cards. Stagger shouted greetings at them, and they all leaped up and responded with their own.

Big Eddie Masters, wearing a black suit and tie emerged from the crowd. He clasped Two Tone's hand with his dinner plate sized appendage and shook.

"Thanks for finding Mr. Lee," he said. "I owe you one."

The handshake tightened in a vice grip. Two Tone

returned the favor. Eddie Masters was a tough punk back in the day, but now he was just a stooge for someone like Stagger. He might be clever, but he was never particularly smart. They locked stares before Masters removed his hand.

Two Tone smirked. "Think nothing of it."

"I'll give you a ride back to your place, Two Tone," Stagger said with a smile. "What about the girl? Where's she going?"

"She's with me," Two Tone replied without pause. She was not going with Stagger Lee. "I need to know about A-Rail. Did Sarpedon's goons say anything?"

Stagger Lee blanched, and his men fell silent at the name. The celebratory atmosphere had all but dissipated. Even Masters turned green. The club owner forced a laugh.

He leaned over and whispered to Two Tone. "A-Rail isn't with *him*. He's with a man named Templeton."

Two Tone grimaced at the name. That was one of the names mentioned in the warehouse.

"Oh, you know him?" Stagger raised his voice and rejoined the crowd. "Don't worry about that. As a form of thanks, I'll tell you what I know about all this. Just . . . give me a few days, alright? I need to get my affairs in order after that unpleasant experience. I owe you one after all."

Two Tone nodded, and Stagger wandered off. The group were now growing rowdy.

Aurora had been staring at Two Tone for some time, but he tried not to notice. She could only be thinking the same as him: this night couldn't get any worse.

And yet, as the police cars illuminated the night-capped

streets, he began to doubt that that was true. A-Rail was still out there, as was Sarpedon, and now he was back in with Stagger Lee. Then there were the cops.

Suddenly death didn't seem so bad.

Chapter 5
"Two Tone and Aurora"

It was three in the morning when Two Tone entered his apartment alone. He crashed in bed and didn't move until his alarm went off three hours later. The sound of a whirring drill went off in his skull, raising him once more.

The lyrics to an old Blues song came to him: *If I Had My Way I'd Tear the Building Down*. There were few titles he agreed with more.

The shower relieved much of the pressure, but it was no cure-all. Pouring water beat the numbness out of his cheeks and forehead while his muscles stung.

Last night was a bust. Not only did he not find A-Rail, but he was back in with Stagger Lee—a man he should have let die, not to mention that the cops were certainly on to him, and he had to go to work. First he did some push-ups, lifted a few weights, and completed a set of sit-ups.

He changed into his simple black pants and suit jacket and combed his white hair. It wasn't necessary to do this since there was no dress code but he would look his best. If you didn't respect what you were doing then there was no point doing it. That was a lesson he learned from Jet long ago. It sure came in handy more than throwing knives did these days.

The job was not hard to get. After he broke from the boys, he began sending in applications. There wasn't much call for anything other than simple office work. All he had to do was answer inquiries and report to his supervisor when the customer warranted it. Two Tone never planned to make it a career, but it was easy money. With it he could pay his bills, buy his Blues music, and be left alone. That was the key. This world had held little meaning once he lost the boys. Fading away into nothing was good enough for him.

But things were different now. While he had no problem living a meager forgotten life on his own, he couldn't just sit by when everything was going to Hell. That wasn't something Jet Boys did.

After eating oatmeal for breakfast and brushing his teeth, he put on his black dress shoes, and left the apartment. All he carried was one chain for protection in one pocket and his key in the other, and yet he felt weighed down. The morning never agreed with him, just as last night hadn't. His muscles still ached.

The old woman was not in the hall, which was strange. He could have sworn she had a psychic ability to know where he was at all times. She was always there when he opened his apartment door, rain or shine.

But it was Aurora was standing there instead.

"Good," she said. "You're up."

"I am."

"I wanted to thank you for last night. You helped me, even though you didn't have to. You even introduced me to Lorraine who let me stay here. I really don't know how to make it up to you."

She was wrapped in a thick woolen blanket from head to toe, and her tawny hair curled around her cheeks and soft lips. Her smile forced its way out, causing his words to stumble. Out of those clothes as if she had transformed from a peasant to a queen.

"Go get some sleep," he said. "And, uh, don't worry about shooting that monster. If it wasn't you, I would have taken his head off like I did the other two."

Her soft eyes watered lightly. "Thanks."

Two Tone didn't feel right about letting the old lady take her in like that. She caught them coming up the stairs and got the wrong idea, insisting Aurora stay with her overnight instead. That old woman always jumped to conclusions. But Two Tone didn't argue. The last thing he needed was more complications in his life. Of course, he was still getting them regardless.

He choked back a yawn. "I'll be back later. I've still got bills to pay. We need to lay low for a few days, before Stagger finally gets back to me about this Templeton cat. Then I'll help you find a place of your own."

"Okay," she said. "But aren't you tired after last night? I'm barely standing as it is."

"I've been through worse. Now go to bed, and tell that old lady to stop listening behind the door."

"Ungrateful boy!" a familiar voice said from the apartment.

He waved goodbye and went off to work, the steel-grey skies of Achaea waiting for him.

And the next three days followed just like this. He would wake up, find Aurora outside his door, and she would talk his ear off about one thing or another. And every time he saw her she was wearing nicer clothes thanks to the old lady and looking more alive. On the second day she packed him a lunch, and on the third she asked him to visit after work. It was hard to resist such a pretty girl.

But he had to. He wasn't going to play around while waiting for Stagger's call. A friend was still in trouble.

Meanwhile, Two Tone went to work. His job was easy; he answered e-mails for customer support. Since just about every other employee worked from home except his pudgy boss, Two Tone had enough time and free space to do some research of his own online. He used his spare time to look up Sarpedon, Templeton, mud men . . . and ball lightning.

There was little to find. Achaea's history was surprisingly straightforward, but even after landing over five hundred years, there was still much cats hadn't figured out. The shadow continent the Central had been built on was surrounded by a nearly endless sea which was itself bordered by a large landmass known as the Frontier across the planet. The Frontier had no information on it, because no one who went there ever came back. Most figured the Leader and the government suppressed information, but some, like Two Tone were more interested in Earth.

Earth itself was a nebulous concept. That was where

people came from, that was where his home was. There were varying opinions on what Earth was like—some said it was a rotting ball of dirt and mud huts, and others were certain it was a paradise they were forced out of—but no one knew the truth. The records had been tampered with, which led to a war—so much was lost and destroyed. It had been so long since they arrived on Achaea and the other ships had left for greener planets, but the debates raged on. Achaea was chosen to be inhabited because it had a similar size and climate to Earth, two moons aside, but that didn't mean there weren't strange things living in the shadows biding their time. Unfortunately, there was no real way to know.

Despite his disappointing research, he did find one thing.

Cities were typically blocked from viewing each other's newsfeeds, but it wasn't impossible to find. Security everywhere had been withering fast over the decades he had been alive, and there was much that leaked out to the populace. There was a report of a mob massacre in Ganymede. Criminals went missing; cops were killed. Some were never found, and others had offed themselves in suspicious manners. This went on for two months. Then, it just stopped. At this same time, strange cult activity was rumored, but none proved.

And that was it. Ganymede had been a mess of random and violent crime ever since.

When the weekend ended, he was grateful. He hadn't had much rest since the night A-Rail vanished, though he squeezed in some naps on his breaks. He wouldn't get much rest this weekend either. Stagger Lee owed him answers.

Though he wouldn't object to seeing more of the girl beforehand.

For the first time all week, it wasn't Aurora waiting for him but the old woman. She was wearing a white summer dress that was hundreds of years out of date, her grey hair done in curls, and a look that almost made him see beyond the wrinkles to the woman she was in her youth. Her gentle smile disarmed him.

"Good afternoon!" she chirped.

"Thanks," he replied. "You . . . too?"

She outstretched a finger and bade him closer. "You must see this."

Two Tone followed her inside. The last time he was in her apartment, he was eighteen years old, and her husband had just died. Things hadn't changed much since. Old green wallpaper and an antique décor of oak end tables, handcrafted chairs, and large lamps, which were made from designs from old books of Earth, all reminded him of his childhood.

From the entranceway he spotted a girl on the balcony. Smooth legs that let him forget his troubles, small bare white shoulders built for clasping, a light blue summer dress flowing in the breeze, and familiar auburn hair stopped him in place. Before he realized it was Aurora, he was already straightening his tie.

The old woman chuckled. "She cleans up well, doesn't she?"

Few understatements were as grand. "Definitely."

"Well, go talk to her. She's been waiting all day for you."

He found the urge to walk and crossed the apartment, swerving around the antique coffee table and leather couch. He slid the glass door open and joined her on the balcony. A wry grin sprouted when she spotted his suit.

"Were we both dressing to impress?" she asked. "No matter how many times I see it, you do look good like that."

The wind blew warmth across his face as he leaned against the balcony railing beside her. "Me? It's just the same suit I wear all week. You're the one who's stunning. Why did you go and cover yourself in all that garbage for? What a waste."

"That," she said with a joyous smile behind sad eyes, "is because I was hiding."

"From Sarpedon."

"He doesn't know I'm here. I want to make sure he knows who it is that is putting the bullet in his head, so I'm biding my time."

"Ganymede, right?"

"You looked it up." She nodded, and followed his stare out over the barren street below. Even the afternoons were dead in his neighborhood. "Yes, that's where I'm from. I'm the only one who knows what he is, and the only one left to stop him. Nobody knows the truth." She ran her blue eyes over his arms and shoulders. "Other than you, that is."

"Ever come across any cult activity? I hear they're on the rise these days."

"I think that might be what brought Sarpedon here."

He scratched his chin. "You don't think he's some kind of alien, or something that crawled out of the sea?"

"Maybe I watched too many ancient Earth films, but no. The way he acts is far too insidious to be some kind of impartial observer to humanity."

"You're a fan of Earth? That big Earth-lover fad died a while back. No one talks about it these days."

"My mom had a collection of incredibly aged black and white movies. I used to like to watch the ones with the tough guys who got the girl."

Two Tone laughed. "Real life doesn't quite work out that way. But, yeah, I like those movies, too."

"Looks like we have much in common."

"What's it like in Ganymede? Mob towns have to look nicer than this. Cordova must be a disappointment."

"No, it isn't much different. I could look out over a forest of old buildings just like I can here. I can picture the same clouds on my canvas that I see here. The only difference is that Sarpedon hasn't finished with this place yet. Ganymede is a warzone."

"From what I can guess," Two Tone said, "Sarpedon likes to come into town, wipe out his competition, and then slowly take over. But then why didn't he stay in Ganymede?"

She tapped her fingers on the balcony like piano keys. "He's working his way closer to the heart of the Central. He doesn't care about any one city. His goal is to take out the Leader and run things from there. Leaving chaos in his wake helps distract anyone trying to follow him."

Two Tone turned around and leaned with his elbows on the railing. The old lady waved to him from the apartment. It had been ages since she was like this. He waved back.

"Monsters," he said to the girl. "I thought there were no other lifeforms like us on Achaea. We even had to breed our own animals when we first arrived. The planet was empty."

"I don't know what they are, but they're definitely monsters. Especially Sarpedon."

"He's turning people into freaks like him. He's the original." Two Tone nodded as if his deduction made sense. "But there are two other things I need to know about, Aurora. You need to tell me the truth now. This might help me get closer to my friend. Alright?"

She took a hard breath then drum rolled her slender forefingers. "I owe you that much."

"Those mud men. They smell like death; they have bodies hard as stone; and their heads are bent in like their skulls gave out. What exactly are they, and why were they after A-Rail?"

"The Clay Men?" she asked. "That's hard to explain. You might have heard about it on the news a few months back about that mob boss, Orion Verdant, being thrown from the second story of his home. Many of his men are now following Sarpedon. Do I have to say more?"

"So they joined up with the winner. Makes sense."

"Not all of them. The ones that defected were hunted down—and forcefully turned. If that mud gets into your system—"

"It eventually takes control," he interrupted. "I know."

She blinked. "How did you know that?"

"Green Eyes." He still knew nothing about that woman. "Know who that is?"

"I've never heard that name before."

"Worth a shot. But, go on. Is Sarpedon targeting old gang members in Cordova? Is that why they took A-Rail? He thinks we're a threat?"

"The Clay Men are under Sarpedon's total control. You would have to ask him."

"Right." That would be quite the endeavor. "So who is the guy in the black suit—this Templeton kid? He was the last thing I saw before I went under that night. He mentioned Sarpedon."

"I don't know the name. That's something Stagger Lee said he would tell you about, didn't he?"

"He did, but I'm still waiting for him to get back to me. If I don't hear anything soon, I'll be paying that hound a visit."

Stagger Lee had heard Two Tone's story about A-Rail's abduction, and barely reacted to it. People had been missing for months, so it wasn't too strange. Even mentioning monsters didn't faze him. But he did have news that made Two Tone both excited and skeptical.

Two Tone licked his lips. "Before we left the other night, I talked to Stagger once more. He said a square-looking kid in a black suit sometimes showed up every other night for a drink in one of his clubs. But that could be a lie—he didn't even tell me which club. You never know with Stagger. I'm surprised I bothered rescuing him."

"I'm not. But I do wonder. What kind of name is *Two Tone*?"

"I could say the same about your name. Don't think for

a second I believe that's something a father would name his daughter. Unless he hated her."

She laughed. "You've got me. I used to look at pictures of Earth. Alaska's Aurora Borealis was my favorite when I was a little girl. They're apparently caused by the sun's charged particles which release photons, but I don't think it's ever been seen on Achaea since we landed. Earth is different. It's fascinating, don't you agree?"

He smiled. This girl was alright. "I do. Did you keep the knife I took from Smith?"

"Yes. I don't know why you asked me to keep it. No one is going to find us here."

"It can't hurt to have extra protection. You never know with Cordova. I can't expect you to use that gun again since it shook you up."

"How long have you known Lorraine?"

He blanked at the name, and then it was his turn to laugh. "The old lady? Too long."

Inside the apartment, the old woman had already sat on the old couch. She had begun knitting a blue cap on her lap. It was truly surreal seeing her like this. She waved at the two of them again then went back to her work. It had been ages since he saw her so chipper.

Two Tone loosened his tie. "She lost her husband years back. I don't know if she told you that. The two of them always tried to push their way into my life. Some of the most aggravating people you will ever meet."

"She told me about Christopher. He sounds like a good man. Did he teach you to use that chain?"

An itch spiked in the base of his neck at the memory. He scratched it. "That's a very long and boring story. Haven't thought about him in a while. What did you do with that gun, anyway? Judging by your reaction the other night, you didn't even know how to fire it."

"Stagger Lee took it from me. Said he would throw it in the incinerator."

That wasn't good. Stagger never did anything without expecting reciprocation. It wasn't like saving his life would change that. Years of experience had proven Stagger Lee to be a manipulative skunk. But she didn't know that yet.

Two Tone merely smiled at her words. "If you say so. I'll just have a talk with him about that, too."

"We should go inside," she said. "Lorraine wanted to teach me to play a game."

"That old lady never stops."

"Oh, come on."

The old lady dragged them to the small kitchen table. The creaking wooden monstrosity was just small enough to fit the three of them. Two Tone mumbled as he shifted uncomfortably in his chair.

She set up a long wooden board filled with small holes along three rows and pegs which settled inside. He laughed and Aurora glanced at him and then at the ancient crone.

"What's wrong, boy?" the old woman asked. "Too cool to play Cribbage, or have you still not gotten over the last time I skunked you?"

"I was over the skunk line, and I was eleven! I'm pretty sure you count cards, too."

Aurora leaned in. "What is he talking about, Mrs. Cochran?"

"It's pretty simple, sweetie." Cribbage was not easy to explain. Each player is supposed to cut the cards and whoever drew the lowest number got the crib and the first deal. The old lady won and dealt five cards to each of the three players and placed one face down on the side. "It changes with how many people you have, but the important part is the crib. The player with the crib gets two hands to play each round and has the advantage. Each of us has to throw one card in it before we start."

"It's been awhile," Two Tone interrupted. He had to go over the rules in his head. The first part of the game involved each player taking turns playing cards to get to twenty-one. That was the simple part. "You get to move your peg down the board if you get fifteen or twenty-one, or you double a card someone else plays."

Aurora's frown deepened. "This is quite confusing."

"It's easy when you get going," the old lady said. She waited for Two Tone to play first. "So, boy, when were you going to tell me about how you met this sweet girl? She's a much better class than the last tramp you brought around."

"Oh?" Aurora winked at Two Tone. "And who was that?"

He played a six. "You better not tell her, old woman."

"He went out with this one who was so simple you could pour the bay into her empty cavity. This stuffy-faced redhead went on about her clothes and this old musician who wrote vapid songs about pretty girls, and that was it. But she was apparently a good dancer." When it was her turn she put down a three. "Twenty-one, boy."

He watched the old lady take her points and grimaced. "Good dancer, yeah."

Aurora cocked her head. "Sounds like a charmer."

"Would you like to sit around watching forgotten movies from some distant ball of dirt?" the older woman replied.

Aurora and Two Tone shared a glance, but said nothing. He held back a grin. The girl let out a soft laugh.

The old lady continued as if she didn't see them. "Christopher used to talk about girls like her. No sense. No foresight. The stupid boy saw something in her that wasn't there. He's too optimistic. You ever heard about grey cats at night?"

"No," Aurora replied. "What do cats have to do with it?"

"Nothing." Two Tone threw down a five. "Grey cats are hard to see at night. That's all. Means everything blurs together in the dark. In Cordova, you never know what anyone is like, because everyone keeps to themselves. The weather's always crap, and no one goes out if they don't have to. No one knows anything about anyone so no one can be trusted. His stupid saying could mean anything. The old man was crazier than her."

"Oh, quiet, boy," the old lady said, slapping him on the shoulder.

They played their last cards and moved on to the second phase of the game. It was time to count their hands. The old lady asked him to explain it to the girl.

"Now we count up our cards," he said. "The goal is to get as many sets of cards that add up to fifteen as possible.

Every count of fifteen you get is worth two points on the board, so you count them like fifteen-*two*, fifteen-*four*, fifteen-*six*, and so on. Get it?"

She leaned on her elbow and slanted her head at him. Soft hair fell over her exposed shoulder. "Each match of fifteen is two points on the board? Is that it? I really don't get it."

"Close enough," he said. "Just play the game. It's easier to understand if you play."

"This is a weird game."

"It's an old game from Earth." He found it oddly difficult to watch her lips. "Didn't you parents teach you any card games? They were big into Earth, right?"

A beat passed before she responded. "They were more into the art. My parents were odd people."

"Were?" the old lady asked.

"Yes, they've passed."

"Did your father own that .44 Special?" Two Tone asked without looking up from his cards. Only three fifteens. He took his six spots on the board. "That's a good gun for hiding."

"No."

Two Tone nodded. "Then where did you get it?"

"Sar—" Aurora glanced at the old lady, and then coughed. "*Don* had it on him. It was part of his precious collection."

"That's interesting," Two Tone remarked. He let the girl count her cards and thought on it. Why exactly would Sarpedon need a gun? That didn't add up. "I wasn't aware you were that close."

67

She said nothing, but the old woman jumped in. "Quiet, boy. It's none of your business."

"Right," he replied. "Count your cards, already."

When the counting was done, the girl got the next deal. Aurora managed a good twelve points from her hand and was adapting rather quick to the game. The old lady complimented her, and patted her slim fingers.

"So what are you doing with a nasty piece of work like this boy?"

Two Tone rubbed his forehead with his palm.

Aurora giggled. "He's my knight."

"Him? Are you sure?"

"How is *that* so hard to believe?" he found himself asking.

The old woman counted on her fingers. "You're not a ladies' man. You fight all the time. You don't go out. You're always alone. You haven't come home with a girl in years . . ."

"Whoa, whoa," he started. "I got sick of the girls around here, and I've been concentrating on my job. And how do you know I haven't brought a girl around in years? Do you listen at my door?"

"Oh, please, boy. These walls are paper thin. I know you used to just sit on the couch and watch old movies and television shows from Earth with them. They never stayed overnight."

Aurora perked up. "Oh? That's interesting."

Two Tone found his palm meeting his face again. "This is why I want to be left alone. My life is not your business."

"Well," the old lady said, picking up her cards, "that's debateable."

The game went on, and Aurora began to get used to it. The power went out once or twice, but it was nothing unusual; it only raised Two Tone's suspicion that the old lady was using it for cover by swapping cards. The game went on. By the end, Aurora had only lost to the old lady by ten points. It was surprisingly close.

Two Tone came in last.

"Skunked again, boy?"

"No! I'm over the skunk line. See?" He stood up and pointed at the board. He was indeed seven points over the line. "I still wonder about you, old woman."

"Want to play again?" Aurora asked.

He looked at the large carved grandfather clock beside the kitchen and shrugged. It was still early. "Sure."

This time the game was a lot closer. The old lady won again, but Two Tone was only eight points behind her. He finally stood up and stretched.

"I need to crash," he said. "Thanks for the game. I look forward to our next talk, Aurora."

She smiled knowingly at him. "Same here."

"Come by more often, boy. I never get tired of watching you lose."

"You wouldn't," he remarked.

He left the apartment and entered his own. Bright streetlights split the black night and tumbled through his curtains. The cloud covered sky continued masking the moons. He did not miss the eerie feeling he got looking at them.

His phone flashed with a message, and he pushed the button to play it.

There was dead air for a few seconds, and then a small voice cut through.

"*Making friends, Two Tone?*" Green Eyes asked.

The message ended with a click. There were no others.

Whoever this woman was, she was patently annoying.

He removed his tie and jacket and threw them on the couch. It was still early enough for some dinner and watching an old movie before he could finally conk out. He removed a container of soup from his freezer and placed it in the microwave. It wasn't much but it would do the job.

Then the phone rang.

"Yeah?" he barked into it.

"Are you really going to just settle down and watch television?" Green Eyes asked.

"I'm waiting for a call, lady."

"You really trust Stagger Lee that much? The White-Haired Wolf has fallen far indeed."

"What do you know about it? Those days are gone. The gangs are dead and scattered. Unless you know where my friend is, kindly tell me or piss off."

"I do know one thing," she said. Her tone darkened. "Don't reply out loud, but there is someone in your apartment."

His eyes darted across the darkened apartment. "I don't buy it."

"In your room, waiting for you. But that's not all. Look out the window."

He peered through the blinds. Movement on the street caught his attention. There were punks hiding behind dumpsters and around corners in the lot behind the apartment. They were watching the windows of the building.

Swears escaped him as he threw the curtain closed. They were all wearing suits.

"Here's your problem, Two Tone," the woman said. "Me or Stagger Lee. Who do you trust more?"

He glanced down the hall to his room, and then to the blinds. His neck wounds flared just as the timer for his soup went off.

"What's your plan, Green Eyes?"

"My plan? There's only ever been one plan, and that's you."

Chapter 6
"Two Monsters"

Two Tone leaned into the hall off his kitchen. The stink of cheap cologne flooded his nostrils, even cutting through the reheated chicken broth of the soup container in his hand. Green Eyes wasn't lying. There was someone else in the apartment.

He slowly bent his knees as he creeped forward, careful not to hit the squeakier boards, and scanned under the door to his room. Muted light from the street slipped through. It was disturbed by the slow movement of shoes shifting from foot to foot. The intruder was against the wall.

Two Tone slid beside the doorframe and held his breath. He slowly turned the knob and listened. Silence. Then there was a breath!

With all his strength, he threw open the bedroom door. The knob and wood slammed against the intruder. A voice yelped, and Two Tone moved in and slammed his bowl of boiling broth, sliced chicken pieces, and elbow macaroni, against the hound's face. The container bounced off the carpet as a scream escaped the victim. There the intruder fell, clutching his eyes.

On the floor lay a wiry man Two Tone's age wearing a suit jacket, black pants, large boots, and long greasy hair. His caveman-like brow was hidden by his dinner plate hands.

Two Tone leaned over his thrashing victim. He shuffled through the enemy's pockets and removed brass knuckles, sliding them into his own pocket.

"Really, Alby," Two Tone said, still crouching. "I gave you that key for emergencies. Breaking into an old friend's house after not seeing him for near a decade is low. Last time I saw you was when we were nineteen. You haven't changed a bit. Slipping in here during the blackouts when the locks were down was pretty smart, though."

Alby clawed at his own reddened face. "Bastard!"

"What's the deal? Is Stagger now in the business of paying cats to off folks who save his life?"

Alby moaned. His hands still mindlessly wiped at his eyes and cheeks.

"Fine," Two Tone said. He fastened his fingers around Alby's jacket collar and pulled him out of the room along the floor. "Says a lot that you think you need to take me by surprise to beat me."

He arrived back in the living room and whipped Alby forward free of his grip. The gangly thug rolled off the old boards and into the couch.

Alby grunted. "You keep in shape."

"Only reason I didn't throw you out of the window is that they're pricy." Two Tone knelt beside his former friend.

"Did you forget how to knock?"

Alby's long rectangle of a face bore scars Two Tone had never seen before. Where there was once humor in the corners of his eyes only bruises remained. His former bushel of brown hair was greasy, and his thick fingers were cracked. Menace escaped his uneasy grimace as he pulled up the collar of his suit jacket.

"How did you know I was hiding there?"

"Your stink. I'm guessing Stagger put a mark out for me, and you jumped on it. You should have brought something better than knucks. I thought you were smarter than this."

"Give it a rest, Two Tone." Weariness replaced vitriol. Alby rubbed the back of his head. "This was a job. I've got nothing against you."

"You've got nothing for me, either. Get out and tell Stagger that he can do his own job."

"Mr. Lee doesn't want you. He wants that girl you were with. He thought she might be hiding out with you—said she was clearly into you. She was carrying something she shouldn't have been."

"That .44 Special?"

Alby nodded. "He says that the one that kitten has is the same .44 Special that was stolen from him years back. What do you know about it?"

Two Tone knelt before Alby and dug into the inside of his jacket. He removed a key, and threw it in the garbage can. That was one problem fixed.

He patted his old friend on the shoulder. "I've got nothing for you, Alby. Call off your goon squad downstairs and get out. You better hope I never see you again."

"Goon squad?" Alby stood and peered out the window beside the couch. "No one here, man."

Two Tone followed his line of sight and realized that his old friend was right. The dregs were gone. "Where did they go, Alby?"

"What are you talking about? I came alone. I don't need anyone to—"

The window before them thumped. A figure had slammed against it. Alby and Two Tone flinched. Glass spider-webbed then burst. Alby swore, protecting his eyes, and fell back. Two Tone leaped backwards.

A black streak bolted into the window. Before the pair, a man landed against the apartment floor, glass rolling off his black suit and hat.

Alby stumbled against the opposite wall beside the television. He mouthed an obscenity. Two Tone fell beside him.

The figure wore a cowboy hat over his square head. He was only slightly taller than Two Tone, but his muscles bulged awkwardly at every angle. Glass stuck in his skin, thin streams of black blood trickled out. Hunching over, his breaths pumped like a bull ready for the charge.

"Graves," Two Tone mumbled.

Dead eyes widened under the wide brim of the hat. "You know my name? It looks like I found something interesting in this rat nest."

"Another visitor. I'm running out of spare bedrooms, Graves. I can't deal with all these guests."

Outside the window, a mist of what looked like steam wafted up. Two Tone grit his teeth hoping that he was just seeing things. He couldn't deal with another surprise.

"The man who saved Stagger Lee; the White-Haired Wolf. Well-built male with white hair who swings a chain. Your reputation precedes you. Don't know how you managed to off three of us, but it don't matter. Sarpedon wants a chat with you and your bitch."

Alby's brow slanted. "Two Tone, what is going on?"

"Either one of your men has loose lips, or Stagger sold me out," Two Tone replied.

"Stagger?" There was a pause, followed by a low laugh from the monster. "Stagger Lee is remnant of the past, as are dregs like the two of you. Sarpedon is the disinfectant for this world you mongrels poisoned. Soon we won't be the shadow planet anymore, but the world our ancestors will regret abandoning us on."

Two Tone clicked his tongue. "So you're an Earther. You think our ancestors coming here was a mistake."

"Not so much," Graves said. "I just enjoy cleaning dirt from my boots. Making lemonade out of lemons. We can create the world Earthers believe in along the way."

"This planet isn't that bad," Alby said. "Sure it ain't perfect, but it's all we got."

"You only say that because you ignore the truth." Graves jutted his jaw out. "This continent is made entirely up of the Central. Coast to coast and everything inside, there's nothing but miles of city with concrete and steel walls in between. We're surrounded by a sea that the moons play hell with. We're safe, but so what? There is no way out. We either band together, or we rot and die."

"There are other land masses," Two Tone said. He inched forward. "There's always the Frontier. The Central is not everything."

"That's where you're incorrect." More fog drifted up the side of the building. It was growing thicker. "Deserters to the outlands are nothing to concern ourselves with. They'll be dead sooner or later. The Central is what matters. It is the past, present, and future, for all of us."

"We live on the shadow planet, Graves." Two Tone spun the chain in his right hand. He inched closer to the monster. "I don't know what we left behind on Earth and I don't know where the other colonists went, but I do know about us. We picked this planet, and we built the Central over the bodies of those who believed in Achaea. We have an entire continent—a history—together, and you'd be hard-pressed to find anyone who can give the name of their neighbor. There is so much to this universe that goes beyond this planet. Scrambled records or not, all the fiction and non-fiction I've seen ends the same way. It all comes down to this every single time."

Graves crinkled his face. "Comes down to what?"

"Someone like me fighting someone like you."

"Spare me," Graves snapped. "Sarpedon is the way to reclaim what we have lost. He can fix it. Once we are perfected—once we unite—we can lift the Central to its true potential."

Alarms and shouts rang out in the apartment hall beyond

Two Tone's front door. Footsteps pounded outside toward the emergency exit. That was when he realized what that mist was.

"What was that?" Alby asked. "People heading for the stairs?"

Two Tone remained still. Those punks outside must have done it. "The building's on fire."

"Oh yes," Graves said, nodding. "The easiest way to flush rats out is to burn their nest."

Two Tone barely saw the big man move. Graves had made three steps toward him in a smooth flowing motion. Two Tone thought and moved. An arching punch slammed into the kitchen table. The wood broke in two, sending splinters everywhere. Two Tone flung his chain once, and then twice. The first strike cracked against Graves' cheek, the second into his chest. The weight left a sizable mark like fractured glass on his cheek.

Graves twisted sideways with the hit. Two Tone hopped back, but he wasn't fast enough.

The return kick connected with the side of Two Tone's head. His neck bent, and he moved with it. He had barely saved his spinal cord. Two Tone slammed into the coffee table and fell across loose splinters and glass on the floor. His shoulders and forearms throbbed, and blood spilled from his cuts.

Alby rushed Graves and threw out punches. One hit sunk a stray piece of glass deeper into Graves' chest. The monster flinched and threw a knee out, striking Alby in the gut. Alby ejected saliva from his mouth, and his eyes bulged. Graves backhanded him and sent Alby spinning to the floor.

"What is this thing?" Alby wheezed as he pulled himself up. Blood trickled out of his scarred lips. "It's like he's light, heavy, solid, and sharp at the same time."

Two Tone pushed himself from the floor, his muscles burning. "He's a Clay Man. Not human. You have to melt 'em."

Graves laughed again. "You sure are familiar with many things you shouldn't be. Now I see why Sarpedon wants your head. You sure you're not a devil?"

"You would know, wouldn't you?" Two Tone mumbled. He whispered to Alby, "Remember how we sent Fender to the hospital?"

Alby smirked. "Yeah."

"This hound might be made of tougher stuff, but the same concept applies." Two Tone clasped Alby's hand and pulled him up. "I'm worried about a couple of friends, so let's wrap this up."

"I must have suffered brain damage on that last hit. You have friends, Two Tone? I never would have guessed."

"Me neither. Now shut up, Alby. Get in there."

Two Tone took two steps toward Graves, and swerved. A fist sliced through the air where he had just been, taking the monster off balance. Two Tone swung the chain, caught Graves' right forearm, and pulled. He kicked out the monster's right leg and twisted the arm. Graves stumbled as his arm bent backwards.

Alby charged, and Two Tone held the chain tight. Graves could not budge. Alby sprang and brought his boot down on Graves' outstretched arm. The clay flesh cracked and shattered as the stomp slammed through the appendage and into the floor.

Graves howled and fell back. Thick black slime sprayed from the open wound where blood and bone should have been. Graves fell against the couch, knocking it off its legs and to the floor. He screamed and lashed out his left arm, slicing against Two Tone's chest and right shoulder. Blood trickled. Graves dove forward, and his claw twisted for Two Tone's throat. The Clay Man's primal scream sent him off balance. Two Tone tripped as Graves fell upon him.

Alby kicked into Graves' chest, pushing him back. The monster skidded across the floor.

Graves slammed his left fist against the floor. Laminate tiles shattered. Laughter escaped from his cruel smile. The wild breeze swirling smoke from outside blew Graves' hat free of his head. The top of his shaved skull was covered with dried black blood.

"Devils," he hissed under his breath. "You're nothing but—"

Two Tone swung his chain against Graves' jaw. Chunks of clay sprayed out. As the monster fell over, Two Tone lashed the chain out again. He wrapped his weapon the monster's throat, and spun behind his back still holding tight. Graves thrashed as Two Tone stood back to back with him. A cacophony of cracks rang out from the neck. Two Tone held tight to the chain, leaning forwards and pulling Graves back with him off the floor.

Alby's boot struck into Graves' skull. Dust and black

blood sprayed over Two Tone's shoulders and onto the springs and stuffing of the broken couch. Graves suddenly felt lighter.

The head of the Clay Man spun free over Two Tone and soared through the broken window.

The Clay Man's head fell five stories. It plummeted through plumes of smoke and fire down to the pavement below.

Graves' corpse flopped lifelessly to the floor. It shattered like a vase, leaving ash and black mud all over the laminate and broken furniture. Two Tone fell to his knee as his old friend wobbled down beside him.

"Damn," Alby said, "the hound got me good." Blood leaked from his chest like he'd been knifed. "What did he stick me with?"

Two Tone didn't even see him get stabbed. He ran to the kitchen and poured a glass of water.

"Drink it," Two Tone said. Alby looked at him like he was insane. "Just trust me on this."

While Alby drank, Two Tone poured a glass for himself and gulped it down whole. He had no idea how these Clay Men worked, but he wouldn't risk it. Alby held his bleeding chest as he stood up.

"I've got bandages under the sink in the bathroom," Two Tone said. "Go get some."

"Forget that, the building's on fire. We gotta go."

"Not now. I need to head across the hall."

"Well, I'll come with."

"You just said it: the building is on fire, retard. Just get downstairs and wait for the paramedics."

They stumbled out into the empty hall where the fire alarm continued blaring. Smoke covered his sightlines, but he could see that the door to the old lady's place was wide open. He left Alby behind and dashed inside.

"Slow down!" Alby called out.

Two Tone slid into the apartment. There was a trail of mud streaking from the middle of the living room down the old lady's hall past the grandfather clock and toward a closed door by the bedroom. Leaning against it were two figures slumped on the wooden floor. It was Aurora and the old woman.

He knelt down before them. Aurora flinched. Her right leg was wrapped in a red stained towel, and her left arm in another cloth. She coughed violently.

"What happened here? Are you okay?" he asked. "Is she—"

"She's fine. She just fainted. I can't move her alone. Help me get her up."

He took the old woman on his right arm, and draped her arm over his shoulder. "Tell me what happened."

Aurora's thin cheekbones held an unsightly shade of green. Her light blue dress was covered in mud mixed with streaks of black blood. She carried a small bag at her side.

"We were attacked by this crazy woman wearing a black skirt and coat. She had skin like rock."

"That would be Lorna."

"From the warehouse?" Aurora shook it off and continued on. "She was swinging around her fancy knife just like those Clay Men at the harbor. The two of us ran for it. She caught Lorraine, dragged her to the bedroom, threw her face down on the bed, and was ready to . . . finish her. So I . . . I got that monster first. I used Smith's knife and I—"

"I get it," he said. There was no point hearing more. Her bare shoulders shook with the rest of her. "Forget that. Tell me why there is mud all over the place."

"That woman bled mud all over me. She got a few shots in, as you can see. Lorraine fainted. I've been trying to get her out of here, but my legs won't stop shaking."

Two Tone quickly noticed that her forearm wasn't wrapped well. He tightened it, and gestured to the door. Smoke was spilling in at an alarming rate.

"The building is on fire, and Sarpedon is one tenacious bastard. More of these things could be out there."

She blinked at the bandage and then at him. He outstretched his hand, and she took it.

Out in the hall Alby still leaned against Two Tone's door. He looked over the old lady, the girl, and then Two Tone, with an eyebrow lifted. He laughed but said nothing.

They flew down the stairwell. Alby was coughing up a storm, the old lady was out of it, and the girl pressed against him as they descended. Smoke gathered in on them even as they reached the foyer. Two Tone kicked against the front door, allowing Alby and Aurora out, and followed them with the old lady still in his arms.

There on the street was the oddest sight Two Tone had ever seen. Several dozen people stood around in clumps and stared at the fire. They all appeared very different, whether fat or skinny, or with expensive clothes or rags, but they all gazed blandly at the blaze. Some looked ready for the disco and others for a punk club. Not one said anything or took notice as Two Tone's group ran out onto the street. He didn't know any of their names, and he'd lived there in that building his whole life. They looked like aliens to him and probably each other.

Sirens screeched over the crackling flames. Alby sat on the curb across the street, and both Aurora and Two Tone joined him. Unlike the crowd, they turned away from the fire.

"Leave the old lady with me," Alby said, rubbing his forehead.

Two Tone looked at him sideways. "Why would I do that?"

"Because I owe you for what I did before, and you have to get out of here. Simple as that."

"What's he talking about?" Aurora asked.

"Same as what happened to you," Two Tone said. "We were attacked in my apartment by another one of Sarpedon's freaks. They're targeting us."

She clenched her fists and turned away from the two of them. At his point, it was well beyond being personal for her. He didn't bother to pry.

Alby groaned and rotated his shoulder. "I've got a question, Two Tone."

"Make it count."

"All those years ago when we were kids; what did you think I was doing while you were dancing with those girls?

I'll tell you. I was making connections, working my way up from a delivery boy and trading supervisor. Mr. Lee might be an asshole, but he gave me a way to work through this dying town. There's a ceiling to all that, though. You have to have realized it by now. The Central is rotting. We've lost something, I don't know what, and we aren't trying to get it back. And whatever we're fixin' to replace it with creeps me out. That clay freak proved tonight proved it. I don't want any part of what's coming. I'm getting out of this place. Is that cowardly?"

Two Tone knelt down beside Alby and leaned the old lady against him. He didn't answer his old friend's question. Truth be told, leaving town didn't seem so bad at that moment.

But he doubted he would be able to do it. Abandoning Cordova was like admitting defeat. Jet Boys never quit.

The old woman peered at Two Tone through slits.

"Where are you going, boy?" she whispered.

"Away, old lady."

She smiled. "But I enjoyed skunking you."

"You would. Maybe you'll get another chance someday."

Lorraine shook her head and glanced at the fire. "My husband always said the moons look down on us like a fairy tale monster. It's a beast looking to devour children who stay out after dark. Christopher was an odd duck. Those moons remind me that this is not on our real home. There weren't any monsters on Earth. Not like this."

In half a century there had been many that wanted to throw away Earth and their history. But their home planet remained a figure in pop culture from radio shows to movies, spread through folk tales and legends. It had little value these days as anything but a curiosity or novelty. Only weirdos like Christopher or Martin had any interest in the place. Two Tone could never know what Earth was really like, but he doubted anything like those monsters lived there.

"Paramedics will be here soon," he said. "Get some rest. We have to go."

Aurora bent down and hugged her. "Thanks for everything, Lorraine."

"Remember what I said, girl," she said with a wink. "Get going before I chase you both off."

Two Tone took Aurora by the elbow and sprinted down the street and into the nearby alley. His muscles grinded as he moved and the fresh rain sprinkled down on him. It would be another damp night. Blackened clouds blew over the horizon as they left the burning building behind. But he couldn't escape the feeling that it would be the last time he ever saw Alby or Lorraine. Thunder roared over the city as he moved on into the night.

Chapter 7
"Jet Boys"

Two Tone knocked on the door, his shoulder throbbing. Aurora was panting at his side and out of breath. After half an hour of threats the rain was starting to pour down. The pair was utterly drenched.

They had already run several blocks, ducking into alleys when flashing police sirens shone into the dark. Aurora's leg was bothering her, so Two Tone carries her most of the way. She hadn't looked him in the face since then. He wondered just what her deal was.

"Open up, Jet," he said to the door.

Finally the door swung open. A square white face poked out.

"Two Tone?" the face inquired.

"That's right, you hound. What took you so long to answer the door?"

Jet wore reading glasses and had his brown hair combed back. The small lines of freckles under his blue eyes had shrunk with age, as did any semblance of him once having been a boy. His leather jacket had been replaced by a long blue sweater and his jeans were now black slacks. It took a moment for Two Tone to remember that this was once the leader of the Jet Boys.

"I was keeping it locked because of the news. Didn't you hear what was going on?"

"Yes, Jet," Two Tone said. He gestured to Aurora. The girl leaned against him, wobbling. "I'm aware. Now how about letting us in before we freeze to death?"

He blinked. "Oh, yeah, right. Come in."

Two Tone ran straight for the kitchen and shuffled through the cupboards. He retrieved a glass, filled it with water and returned for Aurora. She had sat on the old couch in Jet's living room, and had dropped her bag in the floor. Perspiration flushed over her.

He sat beside her and put the glass into her hands.

"Drink," Two Tone said.

"I already did. The rain."

"Do it again," he said forcefully. "It's not a risk worth taking."

She complied. Within a second she downed the glass.

Jet returned with two towels and handed them to his Two Tone. He wrapped them around Aurora without a second thought.

"So, tell me, Two Tone," Jet said as he sat in the chair across from the couch. "What is going on out there? Who is the young lady?"

"Since when did you learn to talk so weird?" Two Tone asked. It was like speaking to an old, out of touch uncle. "If

I told you everything that happened . . . I don't think you'd get it. Let's just say your old pal Stagger got caught up in a spider web of his own making and now the rest of us are being pulled in."

"He's not my friend."

"He *was*." Two Tone watched Aurora place the empty glass on the coffee table across from the couch. She curled up on the arm rest. "Because of whatever he got tangled up in, several people I know have been hurt—including Alby and A-Rail."

Jet's glare darkened. He sat forward in his chair. "Now I'm interested."

Two Tone went on to tell Jet everything about A-Rail's kidnapping up to the moment he escaped the burning apartment. There was no getting around explaining the mud men, so he didn't pussyfoot around it. Aurora had all but fallen asleep on the couch beside him, lying against the arm with her hands folded like a pillow. The downpour continued to knock about outside.

When the story ended, Jet finally spoke up.

"What did you see when you died?" Jet asked.

"What?" Two Tone scratched his sore neck. "That has nothing to do with this, man. The point is that Stagger knows that kid in the suit who took A-Rail, and Sarpedon is after *Stagger*, and both of *them* after the girl. Stagger is the key here. Do you know anything about him?"

"Look," Jet said with a sigh, "I quit working with Stagger years ago. Got clean. I don't deal in that business anymore."

"Don't wuss out on me now, Jet. I know you. You were

the one that sent punks screaming with their tails between their legs. All they had to do was see that dead look in your eyes, and they knew what was coming. They were right to run. Nobody messed with Jet Matthews. I need that punk right now and not, whatever you are now."

Jet pushed back the glasses on his nose and shook his head. "Being alone changes your perspective on a lot, Two Tone. Look at you. You used to scare everybody in the gang because of the way you thought seven steps ahead. I just bulldozed everything like a fool. Now I see you helping a girl out of the storm and trying to walk into the lion's den without thinking. That isn't you. That's me."

"I always help friends. That's never changed. What I need to do is find Sarpedon and cut off his fat head."

"You would," Jet agreed. "But this mess you're talking about is more like war. What happened? Did you find Jesus since I last saw you?"

"What does that have to do with anything? Focus. I'm here because, for better or worse, you're the only friend left in Cordova. And I need you to be *you*."

"And I just so happen to know Stagger Lee."

Two Tone smirked. "Why do I get the feeling that you don't want me here, Jet? Are you hiding something? You've forgotten who the boys were."

"I remember the old days just fine. Your knife throws were almost as good as mine; I practiced for hours to make sure you didn't top me. But that was then. Other than Martin, I always thought you had the best chance of making it out of Cordova. And you're both still hanging around."

"Your point?"

"What are you planning? Why are you still here?"

The two former friends locked stares. Discordant showers of rainfall pounded against the window shutters, but neither of them would look away from the other.

"What am I planning?" Two Tone repeated carefully. "To find A-Rail, to get this girl away from Sarpedon, and to strangle Stagger Lee within an inch of his pathetic life. Why? It's not like I'm a mystery, Jet. I don't see you or the others eager to help out. Hell, I don't even know where most of the guys ended up. Do you? So why are you chickening out?"

Jet said nothing and sat back in his seat.

Ages had passed since they had last met, but Two Tone was beginning to remember why he hadn't seen Jet in almost as long as Alby. They never did see eye to eye. Jet was a monster in the old days, demolishing everyone with fists harder than titanium and a laugh that could curdle milk. Two Tone preferred plans, and the others never liked that. Jet was the leader because he could beat anyone. The passing of years doesn't change a man's soul.

Two Tone coughed into his fist. "Why did you quit working for Stagger, anyway? Wasn't it your dream gig to fight all the time? You didn't have us to hold you back."

"It was. *Was*. I'm not in with that scene anymore."

The rain was coming down harder outside making it harder to hear his old friend. Two Tone stole a glance at Aurora. She was out of it, and her breaths were slow, but at least she was in one piece.

"Hey, Aurora," he said. No response. "Hey!"

Two Tone braced and leaned her forward. She began to heave uncontrollably. Jet sprinted into the kitchen. The old leader had thrown open the closet door, and within seconds returned clutching an old grey square mop bucket.

The girl coughed relentlessly. She bent forward, and choked. A black mass of sticky mud the size of a fist fell between her soft lips and plopped into the bucket below. Aurora groaned and fell back on the couch. Both Jet and Two Tone stared at the black mud she left behind.

Deep dark muck harmlessly sloshed around in the receptacle. Light reflected off of the murky substance, accentuating the impression that it had no proper texture or solidness to it. It was like a physical manifestation of the Abyss. Thicker than water but thinner than blood, the stink of rotting flesh was stomach-churning.

Aurora finally sat up and followed their stares to the bucket.

"What is that?" she asked with a slur of words.

"It's how the Clay Men spread their disease." Two Tone thought for a moment. "But for some reason I didn't cough anything up. Is it because I didn't swallow it?"

Her mouth parted as if a thought clicked into place. "It must spread faster through the mouth than directly through the blood. This is disgusting. What exactly is this mud?"

"What are you two talking about?" Jet asked. "What is that gunk? What happened to her? And what does it have to do with Stagger, and the boys?"

"You tell me. I've been hiding out with this girl for days now slinking around for information and finding nothing.

I'm getting more than a bit tired of it. This is why I'm asking you about Stagger. How is he involved, Jet?"

Jet stared at the black mud with a stiffened jawline. That was how he looked when puzzling a thought out in his head. It wasn't something he did often back in the day.

"I'll make some calls," he finally said. "If this involves the boys, I'll find out. For now, you two get some rest. She can sleep upstairs. You sleep on the floor."

Instead of waiting for a reply, Jet turned and left them for the kitchen. Two Tone chuckled.

Aurora wheezed. "He believes all this?"

"Jet has no imagination, so I doubt it. But he also doesn't lie." Two Tone hoisted her up off the couch by the arm. Her light, slim frame fell against him. "Come on, let's get you settled."

"Do you actually trust him? This doesn't add up. He's hiding something."

"Don't worry," he said. "Jet is a complete psychopath. Just wait until he puts on the brass knuckles. But you can trust him. That's why I brought you here, after all."

"You're different." Her tired eyes locked onto his. "You're not like him. Or me."

He grinned down at her. "Flattery is a waste of time."

Two Tone helped her ascend the stairs. The warm press of her soft skin against his made it hard to concentrate. The timbre of her voice was as easy to get lost in as her scent. She was gorgeous, and she knew it, but there was something hiding under the surface. He couldn't put a finger on what it was. As much as he wanted to trust her, it wasn't easy.

She wasn't like Jet, A-Rail, or the boys. What you saw was always what you got with the Jet Boys. Aurora was a woman, smooth curves, soft skin, delicate voice, and all. He found it hard to tear his gaze away. The boys never would have stopped talking about her.

But there was no more gang. There were only scattered individuals reliving the glory days in their minds—the ones who remained, that is. Everyone else had moved on just as the rest of the gangs had. The city was going extinct. Cordova might kill itself, but Two Tone wasn't going to just let it happen. He wasn't going to hide anymore. This city would get one more glimpse of the White-Haired Wolf, and they would wish they had just let this dog lie.

Never underestimate a Jet Boy.

She looked up at him as they reached the top step. "What are you chuckling about?"

"Nothing," he said, holding her tight and steady. "Thinking over where we're going to go dancing at when this is all done."

A light breeze of a laugh escaped her. "Maybe I was wrong about you," She said with a wink.

He led her to the bedroom and watched her fall upon the small bed. She went out like a light in seconds. Sirens went off blocks away in between sounds of endlessly falling rain. Thank God she was away from all that. He placed the nearby blanket over her, and left her to sleep in peace.

Two Tone descended the stairs back toward the living room. There were old pictures of the gang on the wall in between a painting of what Earth was supposed to look like—green meadows and plains that went on forever—and some religious pictures. Jet had gotten so clean it was scary. Swept floors, dusted walls, and Jet's old man clothes were not things Two Tone expected. If it wasn't for his scars and roughed knuckles, you would never be able to tell Jet was a demon.

The living room light was oddly dim when Two Tone returned. Jet was sitting in his chair reading a small book with his glasses on. He didn't look up.

"She's sleeping," Two Tone said. He leaned against the archway. "Since when do you read?"

"Since when did you get clean?"

It was like he read minds. Two Tone chuckled. "Years back. You?"

"Same. If the boys saw me next to little old ladies in Church they'd laugh me out of town."

"I know the feeling. There's this one old lady who used to follow me to Mass. She was a pain, always jabbering on and on. Neighbors can be pests. But speaking of the boys— do you keep in touch with them?"

Jet placed his book on the coffee table and removed his glasses. "Martin fell in deeper with Rocks, Scotty's into some real sick stuff, and you already know about Alby. Everyone else is either dead or left town years back. To be honest, I expected you to be dead by now. No offence."

"None taken. Great minds think alike. How much a connection do you still have to Stagger?"

"Well," Jet said. "I don't. There was this hit he tried to make on a hound's life because he wanted the wife. Most of his men kicked up a big stink, including that lump, Eddie Masters. I left and cut off all contact with him. But I do have two pairs of eyes on the inside—Scotty and Martin."

Two Tone groaned. "I should have figured. But you still talk to Scotty? Didn't he try to steal that girl from you? You know Sta—"

"Stacey. We broke up three years ago. It's water under the bridge. Scotty and Martin work at Stagger's Rabid Rabbit club. They're bouncers and pretty good ones. If Stagger knows anything about this Sarpedon, they'll know. I left Scotty a message while you were upstairs. Couldn't get Martin. In the meantime, I really want to know about these Clay Men. Who are they? Where did they come from?"

"Aurora thinks Sarpedon was summoned by some dark cult. I think he either came from the Frontier or the bottom of the sea. Whatever he's made of, it isn't normal."

"You think he's one of those people with powers? The ones from the rumors that show up every few years?"

"No." The certainty in Two Tone's voice surprised him. "Those were goofy things like bending spoons with your mind or floating two inches off the ground. Those were just pranks like those rumors of ghosts on Desoto Street. This isn't some parlor trick. This is some creature from somewhere south of Hell."

"If they want to control us," Jet mused, "then I doubt they're simple aliens. This type of control you're talking about feels more like this guy wants an army he can control on a whim. Reminds me of some of the worst of the old gangs."

"They're more organized than we were back in the day, but we were smart enough to call it quits when we realized knocking each other senseless wasn't going to save this dead end city. These guys want to reshape Cordova, the Central, and all of Achaea into some kind of utopia." Two Tone scratched his neck. "They're no joke. I drowned three of them, Aurora stabbed another, and I took off the head of a fourth with Alby's help. The only reason we beat them was from luck and a lot of effort. They're crazy tough."

"I've never heard of Clay Men before, and I've heard all kinds of legends about the streets."

"They're from Ganymede. All those rumors about dead mobsters? Looks like they're true. Now they want Cordova. We can't just let them take it, Jet. Sure it's a dump, but still—"

"That's enough, Two Tone. You should get some rest. The cops will be looking all over for you, and tracking any purchases you make, so lay low. Tomorrow we'll work on Scotty. He thinks I'm gonna run him down or something."

"You really don't change, do you, Jet?"

His old friend stood up and stretched. "You can sleep on the couch. I gave it a short scrub while you were gone. I'll just rest in the chair in my study. I'm going to call around a bit more, see what I can shake out of some cats."

Two Tone watched his old friend turn out the light, and disappear into the study beside the living room. The door shut, and Two Tone was alone again.

He was starting to get sick of it.

He lay back on the couch with his hands behind his head.

Beams of luminous light occasionally dragged over the shades and washed the room in long curtains of autotaxi headlights. The engines fought against the heavy rain. This neighborhood always had problems with noise.

The last things on his mind were the large green eyes watching him from the clouded sky in his mind.

A familiar voice came to his thoughts. *"Making friends, Two Tone?"*

When he blinked awake again, the morning had arrived. The downpour continued raging thunder and jagged bolts of lightning outside allowing the darkness to envelope the early hours. He rose and found it was only five in the morning.

Upstairs Aurora was still asleep in Jet's room. Her porcelain skin no longer held an ugly tint. Quietly, he left her in peace. Even if she wasn't completely honest, he couldn't help believing her. Women could be annoying like that.

By the front door stood Jet, wearing a navy blue suit, white shirt, and blue tie, with his dark hair combed back. He would have looked professional, if not for the bags under his eyes.

Two Tone yawned. "You look like you crawled out of your own casket."

"That's one way to put it." He straightened his cufflinks. "I was just going to get you up. An old friend of my dad's will be coming to look over your girlfriend."

"Someone I know?"

"Dr. Emily Lowell. She runs a clinic in the neighborhood.

Kinda pudgy and short with curly grey hair. You probably got patched up by her once or twice after a fight."

"Right. Yeah, after that tussle with the Bombers nine years back she pulled some glass out of my left arm." He nodded nostalgically. "That was one crazy brawl."

"Anyway, when she shows, we split. I'm going to meet with Stagger at the Rabid Rabbit, while you squeeze some info out of our old pal. Scotty shares a place behind Archive Cinema with Martin last I heard."

Two Tone glanced at him sideways. "Are you insane? You're going to see Stagger? If he figures out that you have anything to do with me, he'll throw you to the wolves."

"Relax. I'm not bringing any of that up. I have other things to ask him about."

"Such as?"

"Go take a shower and get cleaned up. I put some of my old clothes on the sink. Just roll up the pant legs a bit and you'll look fine. Also, cover your hair—white isn't normal and is easy to spot. Meanwhile, I'll be getting some tickets to the club for the Babylon Rockets show. Stagger won't know why I'm really there."

"I don't need you to help me with this."

Jet ran a palm against his forehead. "Shut up and get clean."

*

Two Tone kept the red umbrella Jet had given him and quickly made his way to Archive. He wore a black cap to cover his white hair and Jet's old black jacket with old jeans with his chain and Alby's brass knuckles in his pockets. Thankfully, he didn't look too out of place in this part of town. No one met him aside from stray cats and the random silent passersby. There were even less people at Archive when he got there.

Pairs of pigeons were pecking at spoiled hot dogs in a trash can. This was the most life he had seen in Cordova in days. Wilting trees were planted along the sidewalk to give the illusion that green life existed here, and purple vines had grown along the side of some buildings in ignored alleyways. Most of the city outside his neighborhood and stomping grounds was very much like this street.

In Cordova there had always been a uniform sterile design to every building. Archive Cinema was no different. Long square boxes with painted grey brick and perfectly perpendicular windows filed in immaculate rows were the same with every street in the area. The only difference with Archive was the long, murky colored, rectangle columns affixed each side of the entrance and the name of the movie on the marquee above. There were no flashing lights, pulsating colors, or decorative posters like he saw in pictures of the old theaters from Earth. Archive only showed surviving films from Earth, but it had no resemblance to that forgotten world otherwise.

A pack of dogs, all thin and bony, sprinted from out of the alley ahead. They darted by him into the downpour. It was rare to see so many together, usually cats were more common than dogs in Cordova. Dogs were far easier to catch. He watched them sprint out of sight.

He turned from the distraction and instantly slammed into someone. A forehead knocked into his right breastbone and recoiled. It was a woman. He caught her as she fell over, one hand around her tight shoulder and the other around her slender waist. The thin woman was oddly heavy.

"Sorry about that," Two Tone said. He let her up. "I wasn't really looking forward."

She glanced up at him, her wide brim hat letting the rain water pour to the sidewalk behind her. A smile as sharp as fangs in her slit eyes met him. Cold daggers surged through his bloodstream.

The woman straightened her trench coat. "It happens."

Chills slithered up his spine. She had a perfectly symmetrical and unblemished face, with no imperfections to be found. Her athletic legs, immaculate breasts, and curvy hips, would have distracted him if he were unaware of whom she was. Her perfect teeth flashed in an attempt at warmth.

Aurora stabbed her to death, and here she was, alive and well.

"You should always look where you're going," Lorna said. "That's a good way to get yourself killed."

Chapter 8
"Return of the Clay Men"

Two Tone steeled himself. This woman didn't know him. She'd never seen or met him before. If he didn't see her in the warehouse he wouldn't even know she was with Sarpedon. This was his advantage, not hers. He held a good natured grin.

"You should be careful in this part of town," he said. "You never know what you might run into."

She put her fingers to her lips and giggled. "Oh, I can very much handle myself, Mr. . . . may I ask your name?"

"Christopher," he lied. "Christopher Cochran. And you are?"

"Lorna." Perfect white teeth flashed a perfect white smile. "Are you a subversive, Christopher? You dress as one."

"That's an odd thing to ask someone you just met. No, I just keep to myself."

"That is no way to change this city."

He clicked his tongue. "Who says I want it to change?"

"Everyone wants change."

"No, Cordova isn't all that great, but there are treasures buried underneath the garbage."

Her pleasant smiled remained, but her right eye slightly twitched. A smooth and unblemished slender right hand slid toward her thigh, and then around to the small of her back. He quickly realized her game. The street was empty; there would be no witnesses.

Two Tone shrugged. "I admit Cordova could use some cosmetic changes. We could stand to have more repairs and paint jobs. The clubs around here are ass ugly. It's like going dancing in a grocery store. Do you go dancing, Lorna?"

The hand behind her back paused, lingered. Her head slanted. "I cannot say that I have."

"I've got a friend who owns a club called *The Poppin' Perkins*. Ever been? Anyway, they play the best music you could ever move your feet to. Very tight bands. Really get you moving."

"Are you propositioning me?" Her pupils danced around his like a lioness on a gazelle.

There was nothing about her that felt right. Her curves were perfect, as were her breasts. If he were younger, he might go for it. But she gave off a scent under the perfume that was anything about sweet. The thought of a doll was all that came to Two Tone's mind. This woman wasn't real. Of course she also wasn't anywhere near close to . . . why was Aurora coming to his mind again? The warmth in her touch, the perfect corners at the edge of mouth when she smiled . . . but this wasn't the time.

He shrugged at the woman before him. "There isn't

much else to do around here these days. Why not try dancing?"

"Surely you can't abide this filthy swamp. I haven't been here that long, but I simply cannot get accustomed to the stink. It is an embarrassment to civilized people."

Two Tone curled the corner of his lip. "Oh, you're from out of town! Somewhere fun?"

The smile in Lorna's eyes deadened. "We have wasted enough of each other's time. I will have to reject your generous offer. Good day, Mr. Cochran."

The woman hastily shuffled down the sidewalk as rain danced from her hat. Her robotic movements betrayed any attempts at womanly grace. Before he knew it, she had vanished around the corner.

He thought about following her, but it was too risky. These monsters were too much one on one, and he was still feeling his wounds from the previous night. However, if she was in this area then there was a good chance it was for a reason, like she was here to see someone.

Scotty.

"Bastard," Two Tone whispered.

Beyond the storefront of Archive Cinema was the narrow side alley he was looking for. The desolate row of buildings were all boarded up and forgotten, failed businesses from those who had long left for greener pastures. Cement sat broken and split with pale grass betwixt the fissures. This place was the future of all Cordova: a ghost town.

Then he came upon the crumbling wreck of a two story building. The remnants of an old wooden door had been left clinging to the hinges. He knocked and waited.

A dirty round face covered by a greasy mop of black hair peered out. Two Tone instantly recognized the long diagonal scar from forehead to chin on the punk. Scotty wore torn and dirty jeans with an old flannel shirt that hadn't been washed in ages.

The hound looked Two Tone up and down. "Oh, hell."

"Nice to see you again," Two Tone said.

The door swung closed, but not before Two Tone kicked it. Scotty jumped backwards, and the door missed him and slammed against the wall. Paint chips leaped from the impact. Two Tone charged forward, and punched Scotty just below the ribs. His old friend wheezed and dropped to the dirt-covered floorboards. Two Tone shut the door behind him and wiped his hands clean.

Burnt plaster and dust stained everything. The hovel was an antique store years ago, and one that Two Tone had bought his old Blues records at. However, it had gone under four years ago after the owner was stabbed and left to bleed out. It had been abandoned ever since.

"Alright," Two Tone said, massaging his knuckles. "I've got a few questions."

Typical idiot he was, Scotty presented his middle finger in between chokes.

Two Tone removed his cap and tucked it behind his back, revealing his white hair. "I have so very many questions for you, cat. Here's hoping you aren't still stupid. Why did Stagger Lee send Alby after me? What do I have that he wants?"

"You know something?" Scotty growled. "I've always hated you, Two Tone."

"What was Lorna doing here? I saw her coming from this direction."

Scotty's eyes hardened. "Keep her out of this."

"What's Stagger's game, Scotty? You work with him. You know."

"You've always gotten on my nerves." Scotty leaned back against the wall to stand up. "Stagger wants that girl you were with. She had that gun, right? Got lucky and shot someone? He wants to know where she got it from. Alby just went straight to your place like a fool instead of bringing some guys to mess you up. He thought you had a brain and could be reasonable. Alby is one dumb cat."

"Why didn't Stagger just ask her when we saved his life?"

"He was in front of company, right? We also have a traitor, and no idea who. Some dumb cat sold him out and got him snatched. Stagger doesn't do things without a lot of thinking. He doesn't know who to trust right now."

"Something tells me you're not one of the men he trusts." Two Tone stepped in front of his old friend and leered down at him. A stale stench of burnt plant remains wafted from the loser's mouth. "Stagger is a coward, Scotty. He was probably scared of what she meant for him."

"Stagger Lee? Scared of a bitch? Get real."

"No, not a bitch, but because of where she'd gotten that gun. You know the legend he plays off of. He's the only cat in Cordova who ever shot a hound in public, with a club full of witnesses, and got away with it. Even the scanners couldn't catch him. All because the murder weapon, and evidence vanished. The cops had to let him go because of faulty testimony, and the corpse had no bullet. The autopsy couldn't even tell how he died, even though so many people saw him shot. He got away scot-free. That gave him serious cred."

"And what does this have to do with the bitch?" Scotty asked.

"Someone took that gun. Someone held onto it, probably hoping for a favor later. But it ended up in the hands of that girl. And do you know where she got it from?"

Scotty glanced to the hallway to his right and remained silent.

Two Tone continued. "She got it from a man named Sarpedon—a cat who is trying to take over this town. A living, breathing monster. He must be the one that took the .44, and the one who tampered with the entrance wound on 'ol Billy. Stagger Lee made a deal with that freak to dispose of the evidence and scare the witnesses. Now for why *I'm* here, Scotty."

His old friend shouted. Scotty turned, and bolted down the hall. Two Tone kept on his trail.

"That woman works with Sarpedon," Two Tone called out. "Why are you with her?"

Scotty rounded a corner and dashed up a set of musty stairs. Boards creaked under his boots, and dust plumed out with each heavy step.

At the top of the stairs, Scotty swerved left into a doorway and swung the rotting hunk door against his pursuer. Two

Tone charged shoulder first. The wood burst into a spray of splinters and large fragments. He tumbled off balance as he fell through.

Metal flashed on his left. Two Tone ducked and rolled on the floor. The clank of aluminum rang out on the floor behind him.

He bounced back up, and turned to face his opponent. Scotty held the aluminum bat up. Two Tone felt for the chain in his pocket and thought against it. His old friend got stupid when he thought he was at an advantage. It was better to make him think he still had one.

"Never thought you'd be a stooge for a freak like Sarpedon," Two Tone said. He glanced from his opponent to the surrounding room. There was an old mattress and blanket on the floor, a small pile of dirty clothes, and a half-eaten breakfast burrito. There was only room for one occupant. "And where's Martin?"

"Haven't seen him in months."

Two Tone put a hand up. "Put the bat down, Scotty. You know what I'll do if you don't. A-Rail has vanished. They attacked me. Alby got hurt. Martin's missing. We're being targeted. What does that woman have to do with it? What do *you* have to do with it?"

"Get out, Two Tone. Last warning."

"No, this is *your* last warning." Two Tone slipped on the brass knuckles he took from Alby. "If you had anything to do with this . . ."

Scotty's dead eyes widened. "Those are Alby's."

"Put it down."

"Shut up!"

Two Tone rushed in, and the bat darted for his head. His hair brushed the aluminum as it kissed air. Scotty swung it up vertically, striking Two Tone's chin with a crack. Two Tone brought his arm back and slammed his fist forward. His punch landed in the punk's stomach. Scotty gasped and brought the bat down. The aluminum sang. Two Tone's left shoulder surged in agony. Both fell to their knees.

The bat rolled along the floor. Scotty dove for it, and Two Tone followed. He landed on Scotty's back and pressed his knee down. Scotty flailed for the bat but that wasn't going to happen. Two Tone slammed his fist against Scotty's kidney. The punk yowled.

"I take it you know what happens if I do enough damage there, right?" Two Tone asked. "What am I saying? Of course, you do! You've run with me enough times to know. So just answer me. Why is Lorna coming to see you? What do you have to do with Sarpedon?"

"I don't know who that is, damn it! Lorna has nothing to do with it!"

"Does that tingle you get in your jeans come before the lives of your friends?"

"What does any of this matter?" Scotty hissed through his teeth. "It has nothing to do with you. Are you going around harassing the other guys, too? Is that why Stagger wants your head?"

"No, I think I've got this figured out. Stagger threw his weight around, killed a man in public, got cred, and disposed of the evidence. Whoever covered him back then

wants nothing to do with him now. And that's Sarpedon."
It made sense. This was before Sarpedon's current activities.
Things were different now. Of course, Sarpedon would want
to get rid of his competition. "You're the traitor, Scotty. You
work for the cat that is targeting all the old gangs, and the
one who already owns what is left of them. Which one do
you think will be the first to send you into the bay with
cement shoes?"

"We're all dead anyway. Whether it's that Sarpedon guy,
or Stagger Lee, Cordova's done. What the hell do you care
if I make a little extra until then? I have the right."

Two Tone slammed his fist against the hound's kidney
again. Scotty wailed. "I care because my friends are gone,
you monumental idiot! I care because the place we fought
for as kids is dying! Whatever the hell you've turned into is
not what we stood for. Make it up to me and tell me where
they are. At least do it for the friends you've screwed over.
Where is Sarpedon?"

"There's no point telling you. Since when do you care?
You've been hiding out as a nobody for the last how many
years? The White-Haired Wolf is a pathetic old man. This
is what getting old does. Even Jet became weak."

This time Two Tone slammed his knee down. Scotty
yelled again. Two Tone dug into the punk's pockets and
found Scotty's old PDA. It was a black market version
connected to a hidden account—Two Tone once had one
of his own. But he gave that up a long time ago. Two Tone
threw the small slab across the room. It bounced off a rotting
wall.

"Easy!" Scotty said with a whine. "That's my bread money."

"Give me what I want, and I'll leave. You'll never see me again."

"Fine! Sarpedon is looking for a man named Templeton. He ran off from Ganymede with some property of his. Lorna just told me to keep an eye out. That's all I know. Alright?"

"What job do they pay you for?"

His old friend fell silent again and choked down saliva.

Two Tone answered for him. "You give them names and addresses of not only your co-workers in Stagger's place, but *our* names and addresses too. That's why Martin is gone, and that's why they knew where to find me and A-Rail the other night."

Scotty said nothing.

"You sold us all out to a monster for a few black market credits."

Scotty only shook his head.

Two Tone stood up and off of his old friend. Scotty climbed to his hands and knees slowly. Before he could get up, Two Tone brought his boot down on his head. Scotty's skull thumped against the floor. He fell unconscious.

Rage sunk to the pit in Two Tone's stomach. He put his cap back on, and exited back out the way he came. A skull stomping was much too generous for that punk.

The alleyway was as grim as his thoughts. The drizzle had begun again.

A man in a long coat stepped into the end of the alley ahead of him. The stranger's face was covered by a low umbrella over his head. Two Tone stopped twenty feet away.

"You are the one named Two Tone, I take it."

"Sarpedon," Two Tone answered. "Guess Lorna saw through me."

Sarpedon looked exactly as he did in the warehouse. This time he wore a dark green suit and white tie under his coat. His cheeks were perfectly chiseled with a beaming smile peeking under the umbrella. His black hair was smoothed back perfectly with his unblemished skin which gave the impression of a moving mannequin.

"She did," Sarpedon replied. "But let us not dwell on it. We are both busy men with rather long lives ahead of us. Please do me the honor of answering my queries, and I will answer yours. Then we can both move on with our lives and to greater happiness."

Two Tone didn't budge. Two figures were masked in the alley shadows on either side of him. This was an ambush.

"I don't have anything for you," Two Tone answered. "But you can give me one thing. Who is the kid in the black suit with blond hair, and what did he want with A-Rail?"

Sarpedon's smile never faltered. "Now that is unexpected. We were searching for this thug named A-Rail, but he completely dropped off our radar. And you say he was last seen with a man in a black suit?"

"Give me a name."

"Lennox Templeton. A trivial matter, but he has been rather thorny recently. As for this A-Rail, he wasn't taken simply because he was our target. You see, he stole a rather important item from us with the intention of skipping town.

We only wish to settle our business. I thought he was a comrade in arms for the cause, but he was simply another low-life. I have found Cordova to be a disappointment in so many ways. Wasn't your lot supposed to be the honorable type?"

"That doesn't sound like A-Rail. You're lying."

"You never really know anyone, Two Tone. For instance, when you killed two of my Clay Men the other night you were clearly unaware that one of them was your old friend Martin. Who would have pegged you for a cold-blooded murderer?"

Two Tone's jaw clenched. "I've just about had it with you and your whole operation. You're dead."

"Your *town* is dead." Sarpedon laughed. "You never asked to come to this planet of shade and storms. Nobody was ever given a choice. But I will make it a better place."

"By murdering everyone in your way."

"And who have I murdered? A gaggle of insignificant amoeba living in shanty towns? Scurrying cockroaches? A well-groomed rat like Stagger Lee? No one would argue with their uselessness, and yet none of these dregs ever turns away my offers. Why should they? They receive immortality, eternal youth, and a family that will never leave their side until the sun flames out. Not *one* has ever turned me down. I gave your friend Martin a cure for his addition. He could have lived forever. You killed him. Which one of us is the villain?"

"Enough!"

Two Tone ran forward. All he needed to do was knock

Sarpedon down like all the others. Then this would all be over.

The sound of slicing air distracted him. He jumped back. Three crossbow bolts hit the pavement before him. A fourth had struck his right calve.

He tumbled on the cement and landed beside a puddle. The reflection became stained with blood.

Lorna emerged from the shadows holding an auto crossbow. She loaded the weapon and stepped past him. Graves also showed himself out of the darkness. He was alive again! Both clay creatures stood beside their leader once more.

Two Tone gripped the bolt and took a hard breath. He pulled it loose with a firm tug. Skin tore and blood sprayed loose. His scream was choked in his clenched jaw. His leg throbbed, but still he pulled himself up.

Sarpedon was standing right before him now. The smiling man slipped out a small pocket knife, and rammed it into Two Tone's left shoulder. Sarpedon slammed one fist, and then another into his face and chest, and another hit struck his gut and then his ribs.

Two Tone spat air and saliva. The alleyway blurred.

With one hand, Sarpedon lifted Two Tone by the throat, and then launched his victim forward. The ex-punk's brain back flipped as he fell. Two Tone landed against a stack of garbage cans which scattered with the force. Lids banged against the pavement.

He struggled to sit up. A force struck him in the right thigh and then his left shoulder. More bolts pierced his flesh. He bellowed and fell back down.

"So sorry about that," Sarpedon chirped. "Sometimes Lorna is too eager. You did kill her comrades, after all, so you can't blame her. But we aren't quite finished here, Two Tone."

Two Tone took a deep, controlled breath. "I have nothing for you."

"You can pledge me your life." He now stood over Two Tone, a blur of dark patches in the rain. "You were the White-Haired Wolf once. You can be that again, forever. I can give that to you. You don't have to live in this dead city. Just tell me where Jonelle is, and you will taste true immortality."

"Jonelle?"

"Jonelle Verdant. The girl who helped you murder my men. She stole my property, and she is the daughter of a very bad man. I've been looking for her for quite some time. But don't rush to answer me. We have all the time in the world. At least *I* do."

Sarpedon leaned down and, with a single pull, yanked the bolt out of Two Tone's right thigh. The monster tightened his fist, and the bolt cracked and crumbled in his hand.

"While you think it over, I think there is still one more of your old friends I have left to visit. I believe that would be Jet Matthews himself. He should be easy enough to crush."

Two Tone shot forward and met the force of knuckles against his jaw. Stars exploded in his vision. Sarpedon's punch rocked Two Tone backward and into the trash again. The world flashed and flickered between the waterfalls of raindrops.

Sarpedon waved to him, and slowly walked away. The two other figures joined him.

With his last bit of strength Two Tone removed the phone from his pocket and dialed Jet. He might not be there, but Aurora was—if that was even her name. She could warn Jet at the very least. A voice came through on the other end, but he couldn't even make out if it was a male or female. His brain stewed and simmered as he rasped out his location.

"Hurry," he muttered. "Sarpedon . . . coming."

The last thoughts flooding through him were of Aurora, her soft skin, full lips, and her scent. For just a second he thought he could reach out and grab her, holding close. Warmth spilled out of his wounds, but the thought of her kept him awake. Try as he might, he could only barely hold on to the thought of the girl he wanted. Wanted? Yes. Yes, he did. There was nothing and no one he wanted more.

He sat forward, and stopped. His muscles gave and he landed against the cement. The rain endlessly tapped around him until he knew no more.

Chapter 9
"Death on the Shadow Planet"

Endless space surrounded him as he drifted in the midst of piercing pinpoints of light. Supernovas went off billions of miles away, black holes twisted in the back of his mind, and the swirling cosmos went on and on. Earth was an eternity away—but Achaea was below him!

Outer space pushed him away and yet gravity pulled him back. Was he dead again?

Molecules burned and reformed as he fell through the atmosphere. Wind whipped through him. as he plummeted. The Central was miles below and getting closer.

Stars beamed like spotlights through him and down to Achaea as if showing his descent's path. They swirled and merged, spinning like cyclones, until there was but one surrounding him. Two green eyes watched him from the eye of the storm as he fell back to the Central. Inches before hitting the ground, he felt his shoulders shake.

With a blink, he was awake. Aurora was standing over him. Her deep blue eyes brought the heat back into his bones. He would have pulled her close if he wasn't so sore.

"You're alive," Aurora said. She let out a deep breath.

He was lying on a makeshift hospital bed in an old apartment he'd never seen before. Dr. Emily Lowell was shaking her head and standing at the end of the bed. He tried to ignore the odd cleanliness of the grey walls and polished floors, and shook the sleep out. He threw off his heavy blanket and put both feet on the floor.

"I'm only wearing boxers," Two Tone flatly stated. He patted himself down. "Where are my clothes?"

Lowell threw him jeans, and let out a sigh. "There's a white shirt in the wash for you right now. Sorry, but that's all I have. We're not a fashion store."

"Where's Jet?" he asked.

"Still not back," Lowell replied. "Now lie back. He'll be back before you know it."

His muscles ached. He had bandages and patches where Sarpedon had beaten him senseless and his thigh and calve still stung. His abs and chest had seen better days. Even flexing his biceps burned. The wounds felt fresh. How long was he out? Ignoring the wounds, he slid the pants on.

"How long was I out?" he asked.

"One day," Aurora said quietly.

"You should thank her," Lowell said. "She chased me down after I left and told me you were injured. Thankfully Jet told me where you were going, so I knew where to find you. We took an autotaxi there, but since we couldn't take one back, we brought you to one of the old offices near where we found you. She tried to carry you on her own instead of waiting for my son and nephew to show. You can thank them later. Thank her now."

Two Tone noticed that the girl could barely look at him. Shame momentarily washed over him. Of all the people to find him beaten from a fight, it had to be her. There was little chance she wasn't embarrassed about him. "Thanks again. But can we have a moment in private, doctor?"

Lowell looked between them and shrugged. Her chubby cheeks parted with a sigh. "I'll just be outside. Try not to stand up yet. We want that blood to stay inside of you."

She closed the door behind her. Aurora still kept her eyes on the floor. An awkward silence filled Lowell's place.

"Come here," he said.

Aurora sat in the bed beside him. She was wearing a new summer dress, this one shorter and accentuating her slim legs and the blue whirlpools in her eyes. It was hard to look away. Despite it all, she lacked her usual energy. She hadn't slept recently.

"I need to ask you something," he started.

"What is it?"

"Are you Jonelle Verdant?"

The girl recoiled at the name. After a beat, she let out a slow breath. "Yes."

"You're Orion Verdant's daughter. What does that have to do with Sarpedon?"

She stood and moved toward the door. "I'll tell you when you're better. For now, you need rest."

Two Tone sprang from the bed. His calve burned as he approached her. Jonelle turned and saw him coming. She faced him and backed into the door. Two Tone placed his left arm over her flowing chestnut hair and against the wall. He leaned forward. She stared up at him, unflinching. He put his face to hers and glanced into her blue eyes. She looked from his wounded chest and up to his white hair as if examining his wounds.

"Tell me, Jonelle. I need someone to trust right now. You saved my life, again, but you're still hiding things. Why?"

"There's nothing to tell," she whispered.

"Oh, shut up. You're making this more difficult than it has to be. Stop lying."

"I just like to keep to myself."

"You can't do that forever."

"You're one to talk!"

"You know," he said, "I like to look people in the eyes when I talk to them. Especially your eyes. There's nothing quite like them."

She looked up at him again, her blue eyes wide, and her lips slightly parted. "What do you want, Two Tone?"

"You. But how can I when you won't even look me in the eye? So, let's clear the air. Who is Jonelle Verdant, and where does she come from?"

"I come from Ganymede," she said, her gaze never wavering from his. "My parents had extraordinary skills and were well known. My dad was the Shotgun Man. Gun laws are a lot laxer there, but knowing the right people really kept him out of the public eye. He was an excellent hitman. He climbed up the ranks in the family, and eventually headed up the whole thing after some unexplained deaths cleared the way.

"Then he had me. It wasn't until a few months ago that I learned everything about him, and by then he was already dead. Sarpedon, that thing, came knocking, and my dad wouldn't do business. Both him and my mother, and their bodyguards, were murdered in our home. He killed them all."

He loosened his grip on her shoulders. "But not you?"

"No. He never found me. I hid in the panic room behind my parent's bedroom."

"What is his link to your father?"

"My dad was known as the Shotgun Man because of his proficiency with them. He always hit his target late at night in the streets. He was a legend. But he was never caught and tried."

"That sounds familiar." Sarpedon knew all the big players. "But how did you find Stagger's gun?"

"I went out into the gutter and asked around. Followed leads. It wasn't easy with so many dead thugs and cops. Ganymede was pretty shaken over this, including the underworld. I ended up in Sarpedon's place and scraped around for anything I could use against him. That's where I found the gun stashed among knives, bullets, and things that looked like war trophies. I planned to get him with that gun, but he disappeared. Weeks passed before I learned that he'd left town for the next one. I spent the month tracking him to Cordova and trying to find a way here."

"That's not easy. The government keeps a tight watch on who comes and goes."

"Not if you know the right guards," she noted. "These

days there are a lot of apathetic guards who just don't care. You just have to pay them enough, and I used what I had left from my parents. It was simple."

Maybe it was, but he still wondered. For the daughter of a man like Orion Verdant, she certainly didn't act like one would expect. Forceful but not conceited. Playful but not vapid. There was an ineffable quality he could sense but not explain.

He leaned back slightly. "Did you really not know about your father? You had to have been watched by tons of mobsters your whole life, and the cops had to have been by every day."

"That's not it. I just . . ." She ran slim fingers across her forearms. "I just didn't want to believe he could be that man. He was warm at home, at least I thought so. I didn't have a very eventful life. I didn't really trust anyone, I had no friends—no boyfriends. No one ever really looked at me as anything other than his daughter. That's why I watched those ancient Earth movies. That's why I changed my name. I did it all to get away. Don't you sometimes think about other worlds, other places? There has to be something better than Achaea, right?"

"And what are you going to do when Sarpedon's dead? You know you can never go back."

"I don't care what happens to me, as long as he's dead."

"You need to think about the future."

"There isn't anything to think about. If you hadn't found me, I'd be dead. Sarpedon would have killed me. If he never reared his demonic head in Ganymede, I'd still be my daddy's little girl alone in my room. I'd still be that girl dreaming of something better. I never had a real shot at a future. This is the best I can do."

Two Tone sighed and shook his head. "What a waste."

"What waste?"

"A woman like you wading through the muck is a waste. You belong someplace better than that. Just let me handle this. I'm used to being in the thick of it."

"I want you here." Hot tears had begun to stain her cheeks. "Not out there. You don't know what was going through my mind when you called me half-dead like that."

"Tell you what," he said. "If we make it out of here, I'll take you on a date to the best club you've ever seen and I'll even teach you to dance. You'll have a blast."

She blinked. "Are you kidding?"

"I'm not a funny guy. What do you say?"

She covered her cheeks, and rubbed her eyes. "Only if you promise you won't get killed."

"You'd have to ask God about that one. I tend to attract trouble."

"So . . . what are you going to do now?"

"Wait for Jet."

He stumbled backwards and sat on the edge of the bed. His leg ceased screaming. Jonelle waited for a moment before rejoining him.

"If we're going to go out," she said, "I should know your real name."

He smiled, leaned in close, and whispered it.

"Really?" she said. "I never would have imagined."

"Just don't tell anyone. Last thing we need is to soften my image. It's more important than ever that these monsters meet the White-Haired Wolf and learn just who the Jet Boys were."

"So the gang was important to you."

"Yeah. We ran all over putting hounds in their places. Now all that's left is Jet."

"Emily has been trying to get a hold of him. Her contacts still haven't seen him. But what do you mean he's all that's left? What about your friend A-Rail?"

He told her all about what Sarpedon said. How A-Rail skipped town with the help of this Templeton character and wasn't coming back. He'd betrayed them. Martin was dead. Scotty was a traitor. She already knew about Alby. The Jet Boys were a forgotten relic.

"You know Sarpedon's a liar," she answered. "None of that is true. Don't let him get to you."

"I haven't seen any of them in years. Time changes people. I'm different. Jet's different."

"Maybe, maybe not, you would know your friends better than I would. But I know you. I've been watching since I saw you at the warehouse. You've been there for me when you didn't have to. It's embarrassing to say this, but there is no one else I would rather be with than you."

He stared at her open-mouthed. Strange weights lifted from his shoulders and stomach. A bout of joy and terror fought inside of him. He'd never felt like that before: especially not over a girl. By the time he readied to speak, Lowell knocked on the door. The two of them backed off the door and let her in.

"What did I tell you about getting up?" the doctor said. "Leave him be, honey. I need your help with a guest in the next room. He tripped down some stairs, or so he says."

"Okay, Emily." She opened her mouth to say something else to him, but appeared to think better. Lowell led her out the door, and she winked back at him. "Get some rest. We can handle this."

Two Tone slid back under the covers and closed his eyes. Everything inside of him ceased working as if a switch had been flicked and he felt slumber overcome him.

Soon he was back in space, soaring with the comets. But he was still thinking of Jonelle, her unmistakable scent, solid hips, and perfect lips. She kept him from drifting too far.

Two Tone awoke several times from his odd dreams. Every time he did, Jonelle was right there standing over him. Her soft speech soothed his nerves until he went back under.

When the sun rose and peeked through the blinds and overcast clouds, he finally felt the strength to rise again. He found a white shirt draped over the chair beside him and slid it on with his jeans. His chain was in the end table with Alby's brass knuckles. He slid them into his pockets and slipped out of the bed. The old, dusty boards lightly creaked, but the building was otherwise silent. He turned to leave and spotted Jonelle leaning against the doorframe.

"You're really good at that," he said.

"Where are you going?"

"That depends. How long have I been out?"

"Two days. Liberation Day is tomorrow."

"Then so is the concert Jet was getting tickets for."

Liberation Day was a holiday that was as contentious as it was celebrated. The war between the clans and the guilds over a millennia ago was what lead to the fracturing of the people, and construction of the Central. The guilds won and built the Central, their chief becoming the first Leader, whose reign had lasted over the monstrosity since. All this despite civil war after civil war following. The clans had either been assimilated or tried their luck out on the Endless Sea. Many died, but some might have made it to the Frontier, the large continent so far away. Whatever became of them, no one knew except maybe the Leader and his council. Even though the war had ended, the conflict remained in the back of everyone's minds.

Now Two Tone thought more about the Frontier than he ever had before. Maybe those exiles lived. Maybe there was a life far out there that he could have. Maybe with . . .

"Are you alright?" he asked her.

"You're asking me? You really are something else, Two Tone."

"Well, you haven't slept much. Any word from Jet?"

She sighed through her nose. "You have a message on that phone he gave you."

"And you didn't wake me up?"

"The message makes no sense, and you needed rest. But here; take it."

She handed him the small black phone. He found the message and played it.

"Marble Gates," someone said. "Evan's last stop. Come alone. A-Rail's waiting."

That was it. He thought he knew the voice but couldn't know for sure. There was only one way to be certain.

"I don't think Jet's still alive," Jonelle said.

"I'm going now. Cops are probably still looking for both of us, so I've got to do this alone. You stay with Lowell."

"You really don't have to go. You've already done enough. But I know you won't stop until this is over. That is one thing I love about you."

"Only one thing?" He stepped over and gently placed his scarred hands on her small shoulders. "I have to know."

"I get it." She placed her slender fingers across his knuckles. "Just, please, stay safe."

"I'm not too good at that. But for you I'll be on my best behavior."

Her lip quivered, but then she bit it hard. "Good luck, Henry."

Two Tone winked and, regrettably, left her behind for the cold outside.

*

The morning had found its way to fog in the time since Two Tone had risen. The streets were empty as he strained his way down them.

Evan died in a fight with the Firewalkers eleven years ago. The "*Marble Gates*" were what he was talking about as he died there in the street. No one had the heart at the time to tell him that the term was "*Pearly Gates*" for obvious reasons. The voice on the phone was talking about Vincent Street. That was where Two Tone needed to go.

It was only six blocks away, but it wasn't a pleasant place to be. Rows of boarded up homes waited on the roadsides with old food wrappers and empty bottles rolling around. A gang of thin tabby cats ran through a hole in a nearby wooden fence.

He never liked this place. The streets were dirty, but it was the memories that were truly filthy.

Jet had gotten a bunch of the gangs together, and they stormed Vincent Street. It was an all-out war, and the Firewalkers were flushed out. Two Tone made a name for himself at the time, smashing down hound after hound and walking out with the least injuries of anyone. For a long time, that was the best day of his life.

That was a long time ago in an era since forgotten. It was forgotten, that is, except by the cats who wanted them all dead.

The rusty scaffoldings were the same as always, as were the oversized black dumpsters and potholes. Rain puddles stained the pavement under the fog.

At the dead end of the alley where Evan died was no longer a solid brick wall. Now a large chunk had been ripped out for a path to the next street over.

There stood the man Two Tone had been searching for. He wore a black suit with well combed blonde hair and was in his late teens or early twenties.

"It took you long enough," Lennox Templeton said.

Two Tone scanned the boy's slumped posture. Templeton's suit rippled as if it were a pool of black water grafted to his body. Hooded eyes stared blankly back at him.

"You again." Two Tone clutched the chain beside him. "Who the hell are you?"

"We need to act fast if you want to help your friend Jet." Templeton glanced down the shadows of the pathway. "What do you say, A-Rail? Can we trust this guy?"

Behind the nearby dumpster stepped A-Rail, dressed in black clothes with a black cap over his head.

Two Tone's tongue tripped over himself to find the words. But he didn't have time to say anything.

Six other figures dressed in black emerged from behind A-Rail. They swarmed from every angle of the alley as if waiting for this moment. The gang of punks all held bats, pipes, knives, and chains. They all circled around Two Tone like wolves.

"A-Rail!" Two Tone called out.

But his friend did not respond. He remained, unmoving, at the back of the encroaching crowd.

Apparently A-Rail didn't skip town. He simply found himself a whole new gang to play around with.

Chapter 10
"Stagger's Play"

The crowd slowly encroached on Two Tone. Some carried bats, some chains like his, and even some held knives, but he paid Templeton's men little attention. They were muttering insults and jokes and yet Two Tone kept his attention forward on his target. A-Rail was at the back of the group, unmoving.

"The hell is this?" one punk asked.

Another laughed. "One of Sarpedon's hounds?"

"Where have you been, A-Rail?" Two Tone asked, ignoring the group. "I've been killing myself trying to find you."

"You should have stayed out of it, Two Tone. I asked Templeton to bring you back to your home, and he did. We even gave you the water and a note. You have nothing to do with this. Leave."

"In other words, you knew what was going on, and you hung me out to dry."

A-Rail spat on the ground. "No. When I was hired for

the job, Templeton told me all about this crap with Clay Men and Sarpedon, and I didn't believe him. Who would?

"But when we were attacked that night, I knew he wasn't lying. It suddenly made sense as to who caused the disappearances and why some of the boys vanished too. Sarpedon is hunting us down like dogs. There's nobody in the old gangs left in Cordova except us. And we're going to stop him together."

"But you, Two Tone," Templeton interrupted, "you were magnificent. I've never seen a man take down two mud men with only a chain. Then I heard what happened to Smith, Jenkins, and Lazlo. Amazing. I wanted you to join us. But I recruited A-Rail first, and he disagreed."

The mist hovered about the alley like a bad dream. Even the dregs surrounding him had fallen silent. Two Tone wanted to believe this was all just some nightmare, but he knew better. Even if the old gangs were gone, something worse was threatening to fill their place. This Templeton character gave off a rotten atmosphere—as if someone had taken a melon-baller to his soul. Did none of these idiots sense it?

"Two Tone," A-Rail said. "It's only you and me left. Templeton's inside man said that they have Jet. Stagger is planning on offering him as a sacrifice to Sarpedon. I wanted to keep you safe, but I guess that ship has sailed into the Endless Sea and capsized. Will you join us?"

"His inside man was Scotty playing for multiple teams. He's as worthless as putting trust in this shadow man here." He gestured at Templeton. "He's one of them, you know."

The crowd roared in disapproval. Several encroached on Two Tone, and he drew his chain. A-Rail yelled out for calm.

"Come on," he said. "Two Tone is a loudmouth, but he's on our side. We just need to rationally discuss this."

Two Tone couldn't help but laugh. "You always had a way with worming your words, A-Rail. Before any of that, I have a question to ask your pal here."

"Yes?" Templeton asked. His calmness was unnerving.

"Where's Jet?"

"Stagger Lee has him locked in his basement. He wants to trade him to Sarpedon for something he will never get."

"Then that makes my next question easier. What is Sarpedon? How can we kill him and keep him that way? I thought I killed Graves in my apartment, but that turned out to be a no go. He's still walking around."

"Once the mud gets into you there are two things that can happen. You either die, or you turn into a Clay Man for Sarpedon to shape. The only way to prolong death is by expelling the mud in your system. Ingesting large amounts of water will do it, but it has to be taken in voluntarily. I don't understand the rules myself, but whatever Sarpedon is, he is bound by those rules. The substance is very weak at first unless it's allowed to fester. But there are side effects. The ones you met in that alley with A-Rail are one example of it."

A clearer picture was forming in Two Tone's mind. Whatever Sarpedon was made of was the real problem. "Tell me what you want in all this, Templeton. I recognize some of these hounds you got with you. They ran with the Bombers, the Devils, and the Sidewinders. You hoping to fill Sarpedon's place once he's dust?"

Once more voices of disagreement burst from the crowd. He ignored them and focused on the blond haired suit.

"I need you all to kill Sarpedon and end this game. I would do it myself, but I'm at my limit. You see this suit? It takes all my will to hold it at bay so that it doesn't swallow me whole. Time is limited, and he is only gaining strength."

Templeton swung his arm, and a long black claw like an eagle talon leaped from his suit and dashed across the alley brick. Claw marks imprinted on the wall as rubble fell from the building exterior. The suit rippled like snakes under the surface of a deep black lake which matched the stained circles under his eyes. Templeton's limbs shook as if his bones were diseased.

"You understand," Templeton said. "I don't sleep. I don't eat. I spend every minute awake holding this in check. If I let go, this suit will devour me, and I will become like those monsters you killed." He rotated his wrists, and the cuffs bulged and sloshed like rings of sludge. "He did not turn me into a Clay Man. He wrapped my skin in his devil muck and imprisoned me here."

"So you need help to take down the big man. I get that. But hiding like you do is not my style. I want to hit Sarpedon and hit him hard. I want to see his face twist in despair as I crush his throat, and he realizes he will never get what he wants. If you want my help, then you better get behind me or get out of my way. Sarpedon is mine."

Templeton nodded. "This is our only chance to hit

Sarpedon. Tomorrow night is the Liberation Day show at Stagger Lee's Rabid Rabbit club. There he can make a real scene. We know he's after your friend Jet, and that's where he's being held. Neither Sarpedon nor Stagger Lee will be expecting me, or any of you all. There is no better chance to strike. When he gets in there we'll surround the place and make sure he'll never get out again."

"I owe you one for saving me from the mud men, so I won't turn you down flat." Two Tone nodded at his savior. "But you still haven't told me who you are, Templeton."

"Someone who made some bad life choices. I'm sure you can relate. The important takeaway is that Sarpedon is a threat, and Stagger Lee is in his way. He wants to mold Achaea anew."

"He wants it to be Earth."

"Earth!" Templeton laughed. "Earth is a myth. You know that. We can't even find the full records from when we landed on this mudball. What makes you think anyone knows what it was like before we left? The only bigger fool than Sarpedon is anyone pining for a legend."

"We left Earth because we wanted more. More lands to run across and more skies to see."

"Or maybe we just wanted to escape."

Now this was getting odd. Two Tone licked his lips. "Escape from what?"

"Unknown forces. Magic, maybe. Nobody really knows. A Pandora's Box was opened, and Earth was radically changed. The ones that wanted to leave did so. In other words, they were cowards."

"You could be wrong."

"I might be lying." Templeton shrugged. "But I'm not."

"No, I don't doubt the possibility. What I mean was that you could be wrong on why we left. Maybe this magic or force changed things for us. Maybe we found more to the universe than we first thought, and this was the push we needed to leave. Either way, we're here now."

"Exactly, we're here because of someone else's choice. That is what infuriates Sarpedon. He feels it necessary to correct man's mistake."

"So we kill him and things go back to normal."

"No," Templeton said. "We kill him so that no one else ends up like me, or those things you fought."

"If that's what you want. Tell me your plan."

"My plan is to get supplies and men together and get ready for the long night ahead. You might want to get some rest. Tomorrow will be hell."

*

Hours passed, and yet nothing quite settled in Two Tone's gut. He sat aside from the others in the old abandoned bar who were chatting amongst themselves off at a table in the corner. Templeton had led him and the group through the misty morning and over eleven blocks. None of the thugs paid him much mind, not even A-Rail.

He felt sleep tugging at his brain. Despite his rest at Lowell's, his wounds still burned and his stamina was still not back to normal. His phone was in his hand as he debated calling Jonelle. He'd never been so hesitant in his life. The irritation set in as he went over his decision. Then he closed his eyes one too many times.

The phone ringing broke him out of his slumber. He glanced at the time. It was six in the morning. No one else was in the bar. Somehow he had slept through the whole day and night. He answered it without looking at the number calling.

"Yeah?" he asked.

"Am I glad to hear your voice," Stagger Lee said.

"What could you possibly want with me?"

"I just want to talk. All civilized men should talk. You saved my life, remember?"

"I don't care, Stagger. You lost me when you sent Alby and your fledgling hounds after me."

"But I've got your girl," he whispered. "Here, listen."

The phone let out dead air. Two Tone could make out the sound of light breathing, but nothing else. Was someone there?

"Speak, bitch!" Stagger roared.

"Shut your mouth, Stagger. I know it's her." The dumb girl didn't want to drag him into it. Somehow she always knew how best to grate on Two Tone's nerves. "I'm considering which appendages and organs I'm going to remove if you've done anything to her."

"We burnt down that fake eyesore clinic and sent Lowell to the real thing. If we can do that to a dinky little quack doctor's office, just imagine what we can do to your kitten here."

The plastic of the phone creaked in Two Tone's tightening

grip. "That's a hell of a way to ask for a favor from the guy who saved your life. You're not going to like what I do next."

"Tonight at ten, come to the Rabid Rabbit. The Babylon Rockets are playing for our Liberation Day celebration. You'll enjoy them. We'll have fun while we talk this whole thing out. We really want the same thing, Two Tone. Really, we do."

"Where's Jet?"

"He's resting. I've got a seat in the back just for him. Come and join us; we'll all have a grand time. We can deal with this like adults."

"You almost sound reasonable, Stagger. If I didn't know you were such a sociopath I might almost come around to liking you."

"I feel the same."

"I'll be there. You do anything to the girl, and you'll wish I left you dead on that dock."

"Cheers."

Two Tone slammed the phone on the rotting coffee table before him. Rage seethed just under his collar, but he held fast. Control was what he needed—not emotions. The screaming though bored its way into his brain: he should have brought Jonelle with him.

Boot steps pounded the floor. Templeton sat in the leather couch across from him.

"Who were you talking to?" the suit asked.

"Stagger Lee."

"What did he want?"

"Me."

"And you're going to give it to him."

Two Tone swallowed his rage. "You know me better than I thought."

*

The downpour threw itself against Two Tone's umbrella. The cold weather had returned with a particular vengeance. The sticky humidity and fog had been blown out.

It felt and looked like he fell through a garbage disposal, his body still covered in bandages, and his wounds still throbbing. Templeton had given him a grey suit and tie to get into the club, and he took it without any fuss. His borrowed trench coat blew in the wind, shielding his wounds from the breeze. Thunder drummed over cloud capped skies as he tromped forward.

The streets in this area were full of potholes and boarded up windows. Despite the Rabid Rabbit's popularity, it didn't look like Stagger's pull contributed to fixing anything. He was never much of a leader: just a glorified mobster.

At the front door a pudgy bouncer wrapped in tight clothing stopped him. There were surprisingly few people hanging around outside. The large man looked his bruised face and suit over once, took his name, and let him inside.

The flashing lights of the Rabid Rabbit were reminders of his first death. Above were swirling tapestries of stars—pin pricks of light piercing his eyes. The pulsing white lights on the stage, the thumping upright bass of the band, and the screeching guitar like the thunder of Zeus, brought him back further to his youth. Past and present merged for that moment.

There were teenagers and young guys and gals jumping in the crowd, kittens and cats with more hair dye and piercings than sense. Older cats, and possibly parents, sat in chairs by tables on a slightly elevated floor horseshoed around the crowd. The older cats were being served by waitresses who delivered drinks from the bar wearing servant outfits like old time maids. They all wore clothes inspired from old fashion books from Earth. There were bellbottoms, torn denim jackets, tight shirts, and hair styles from afros to bright dye jobs. Cohesion had no place here.

Marble pillars stuck out like sore thumbs considering the otherwise sterile design. Bright lights and big colors were plastered all over the walls and ceiling. Stagger never did have much taste.

Two Tone caught sight of a few men in tan suits watching him from the corners. He kept moving regardless.

The dancing and jumping finally slowed down as the song came to an end. The lead singer, a slightly chubby rocker with a round face and spiky black hair, stepped to the mic and hollered at the audience. They responded in kind.

He raised a fist. "Thanks for coming, everybody!"

The crowd roared. Some teenager whistled through the cheers.

"*If I Had My Way!*" some folks shouted. Song requests flowed out from the large group.

The singer put a hand out. "We'll get to it, guys! I just wanted to say thanks for giving us such a great reception and a hearty thanks to Mr. Stagger Lee for having us for his Liberation Day show. We fought a great war so long ago just so you could have moments like this to have fun and be free. We should be looking forward to the future. What do you say?"

The crowd before him roared. The older audience at the tables clapped.

Two Tone used this moment to slip through. The bodies all sidestepped as he passed. When he reached the rear stairwell, a hand clapped on his shoulder.

"Don't worry, man." It was a younger kid with wild blond hair, a long face, and a sideways smirk. "Mr. Matthews is still in one piece."

He led Two Tone past the bouncer and up the stairs. This must have been Jet's contact.

"What about the girl?" Two Tone asked.

"Upstairs, my man."

"Who are you, anyway?"

"Name's Steve-O. Mr. Matthews helped me out a good deal a few years back when I was struggling. Got me this job, and I owe him for it. Just be careful around Mr. Lee."

"Alright, Jimmy," the singer said from the stage behind them. "Let's rip!"

The tenor saxophonist played a few halting notes before spinning it into a masterful solo. The drummer joined him with a flam on the toms followed by a roll, and then the bassist and guitarist came rushing after. The kids went nuts. These guys were good.

Two Tone crossed the long hall. They passed giant barred windows on his right where the streetlights shone through. Steve-O pounded on the office door.

The door swung open to reveal Eddie Masters. He wore a nice black suit with his brown hair slicked back like always which matched his bulldog face. The big man gestured Two Tone in and slammed the door shut leaving Steve-O on the opposite side.

The office was bigger than Two Tone's living room, with far better red carpeting, decorative lamps, and elm desks to garnish the setting. On the left side of the office was a large window overlooking the club below. The flashing lights were blocked by a thick black curtain. In front of the desk in the center of the room sat a slim woman in a red dress with auburn hair done up and perfect legs. Jonelle turned when she saw him, her eyes wide. She was about to get up when a pair of thugs with tan suits stepped between her and Two Tone.

"Not yet," Stagger said from behind the desk. "We have some things to talk about first."

"You okay?" Two Tone asked her.

She nodded, a grim smile forced its way onto her face. "Yes."

"Get her out of here," Stagger said.

The pair of hounds took Jonelle by her arms and led her out the door. Two Tone held his emotions in check. Templeton had given him a phone and said he would call at the right time. There was no telling when Sarpedon would show, and Two Tone still needed to find Jet.

He grimaced. "You really shouldn't have taken her like that."

"The bitch is safe," Stagger chirped. His black suit and

tie matched his beady brown eyes and coal black hair. His chubby cheeks split into a grin. "I didn't want you to try anything smart. I know you, Two Tone. You're not like the others from your gang of losers. You're dangerous."

"Dangerous is a good thing. It keeps hounds in this dead city from circling in."

"As for your woman, I haven't harmed a hair on her. But as for your former leader . . ."

Two Tone leaned over the tall desk. "I should have let them drown you."

"I'm grateful that you didn't. Sarpedon has come around. You see, all he wants is you, your former leader, and the girl in exchange for my city. Normally I would grind him into sausage for my pups, but I'm sure you understand why that is not feasible."

"Sarpedon messed with Billy's insides, didn't he? That's how they never found evidence of a bullet entry or exit wounds. He completely wrecked your victim's internal organs and skin. I'm sure that mud can of his do all sorts of things to your insides. He made a deal to cover up that death, and you would give Sarpedon what he wanted. How far off the mark am I?"

Stagger flinched, smiled, and sat back in his chair. "*Dangerous* was definitely correct. After the gangs died, there was a whole city for the taking. No one would turn down an offer like that. Sarpedon gave me a foot in the door. Now he comes back and says I've outlived my purpose. Does he think he's God? Well, maybe he is, but I just did what I always do. I made a bargain."

"Do you think you can make a bargain with me?"

"I think you will do as you're told as long as I keep the bitch in her doghouse."

"Call her that one more time." Two Tone flashed a wild grin. "Just say it."

Stagger glanced away and waved a hand. "There isn't a problem here, Two Tone. Sarpedon is incredible. You've dealt with him, so you know. Why wouldn't you want that power?"

"Why would anyone stand in line for a lobotomy you insipid moron? Do you really not get what will happen if that thing gets Cordova, then the Central, and then Achaea itself? We don't even know if there are any other surviving humans out there in another galaxy. Sarpedon could wipe out our entire species. There is no deal here. You either die now, or when he gets to you later. And he isn't coming later. He will be here tonight."

"He's taking over a dead city; he's taking over a dead planet. As long as I can get what I can before he does, well, at least I have that much. Now enough of this idiocy. Eddie will show you to the quarters you will stay in until we ship you to Sarpedon."

Two Tone shifted in his pocket and hit the last name he called. On the second ring there was an answer.

"Hey!" The big man standing behind Stagger stepped forward. "Give me your phone."

He removed the phone and handed it to Eddie. "Say hello to Templeton."

Eddie took the phone to his ear. After a moment, his mouth fell open.

"You should hear this, sir."

Stagger sighed and rubbed his temples. He took the phone from Eddie and listened to the speaker. It only took half a minute for him to pitch it across the room. The phone crunched against the wall and smashed all over the carpet.

Stagger waved at Eddie. "Get this idiot out of here!"

Eddie grabbed Two Tone by the coat collar and marched him out of the room.

Stagger sunk back in his chair, swearing to no one. There wasn't a way out for him. Even as Two Tone was led down the hall, he knew what it was Templeton had said to the fool.

It was a final warning that Sarpedon was coming for his head in mere hours. But Stagger ignored it, and everyone in the building would die for his greed.

Two Tone was marched down the stairs. The band played on, oblivious as to what was about to occur.

The night was still young, but it was already nearing its end.

Chapter 11
"The Menace of Sarpedon"

The basement door slammed shut behind Two Tone as he stumbled in. Before him were rows of cement pillars under a low ceiling to match the drab grey paint, stacked chairs and tables, and a lone swinging light bulb in the center of the room. Unfortunately, Eddie Masters had taken the chain from his pocket and his brass knuckles, leaving him quite naked and exposed. The smell of cheap cologne and stale tobacco was everywhere in the dark room. He had to squint in order to see anything, but soon saw what he was looking for.

The body of a man in a suit lying against a cold cement pillar near the rear of the basement. Cuts and abrasions had stained his face and blue suit.

Jet had been tied with ropes around his arms and wrists, and left slumped over and unconscious. Blood caked in his hair and his left shoulder bulged oddly at the shoulder joint.

"Are you still in one piece?" Two Tone asked. He grabbed at the ropes.

Jet coughed, and opened his right eye. "Who do you think you're talking to?"

"Steve-O told me you were still kicking. You look like they forgot to dump you into the coffin. Can you even stand?"

"My legs are fine. The shoulder was me trying to get out of this place. I was trying to dislocate it to help me squeeze from the ropes. Guess it didn't work."

Two Tone hoisted Jet by his non-dislodged shoulder. His friend wobbled for a second then quickly steadied. Sweat stained his brow. Red teeth clenched, Jet leaned against the pillar.

With as much might as he could, Jet slammed his shoulder against the pillar. Muffled yelps escaped him. He swung again and again. Finally, he stepped back and rotated his shoulder as if it was perfectly healthy.

Jet shook his head and slapped his cheeks. "Good enough for now."

"Lowell teach you that? Anyway, we need to get back to Jonelle before the chaos begins."

"Is that the girl's real name? Well, if you've got dibs I'm not gonna elbow my way in. But enough about that. I tried reasoning with him, but Stagger is an imbecile. He's dead certain that this Sarpedon will spare him, if he just hands him the keys to the city. Speaking of imbeciles, what are you and that girl even doing here?"

Two Tone explained everything that happened since they last met days ago. There was surprisingly little to tell that Jet hadn't already figured out. Martin and Scotty had been written off long ago by the old leader, but he was still disappointed to hear how far they fell. It was when he heard about A-Rail that his interest peaked.

"Who is Templeton?" he asked.

"Some minor threat to Sarpedon. Not quite a Clay Man, not quite human. What I don't know is why A-Rail joined up with him. A-Rail was a lot of things, but he was never a traitor."

Jet laughed low and snarled. "You're never going to grow up, are you? A-Rail is an opportunist. He stuck by us through firebombs and knife fights because he knew we were tough—the toughest. When the gangs broke up, I'm surprised he stuck around town. He never joined up with Stagger, and he went clean. But apparently that last part was wrong. He almost had me fooled."

"But he always had my back."

"Until he didn't. Tell me something. Why didn't he help you when Sarpedon and Stagger's hounds attacked your building? How about at the warehouse? Why didn't he tell you anything after you were nearly killed? He ran and hid. We're all alone out here, Two Tone. If we're going to get the girl and get out, we're going to do it on our own. This Templeton cat won't help us."

"The building is already surrounded, Jet. Templeton's men are waiting for Sarpedon to make his move soon. That's when we strike. That's when you take out whoever you can and go for the exit, and when I go for Jonelle."

"*We*. Not *I*."

Two Tone leaned against the wall, his thigh was acting

up. "She doesn't even trust you, you know. She thinks you're after something."

"Of course I am. I'm a man, just like you. I want to find a place to call my own where no one will get at me. Who doesn't? That's why I formed the gang in the first place. But it's not like I could keep forcing you knuckleheads into it. After all, there's no winning here. We live in the worst corner of the dark planet. What we do is stave off suicide."

Suicide was the right word. Two Tone still remembered all the fights and all the wild times he'd had with the guys. The guys were broken and battered, and yet they kept coming back for more. Youthful vigor can overcome anything, until even that runs out. The boys were all gone. All grey cats faded into the night. Only the two of them were still standing.

"I have a reason to be here," Two Tone said. "You don't."

Jet laughed. "I know. She's a looker, I'll give you that. Personally, I prefer redheads."

"You always had lousy taste in women."

"Maybe. But I'm not leaving. Think of this as the last hurrah for the guys. Alby, Martin, and the others, would love to have been here for this."

"Not if they knew me seeing ball lightning, mud men, and a pair of green eyes started this."

"You also saw green eyes?" Jet asked. "I saw them when I was out of it before. What are they?"

Before Two Tone could answer, a cacophony of screams screeched outside the basement room. A ruckus of spilled tables and loud thumps sounded. The guards on the opposite side of the door yelled to each other in muffled voices.

"And that would be Sarpedon," Two Tone said. "Think you can handle this, old man?"

He cracked his knuckles. "Do you have to ask?"

This would have to be quick. Before the guards regained their bearings it was time to strike. The pair slunk to the door, with Two Tone in front. He took a breath, and sprang.

Two Tone kicked the door to the hall, and the knob broke off as it swung open.

He whirled to the left, surprising the guard positioned there. The suit drew a knife from his belt and swiped it toward Two Tone's stomach. He caught the blade between his palms. The suit's teeth chattered as he mindlessly twisted it forward. Two Tone brought his knee up striking the suit's fingers loosening the grip on the knife. The blade dropped. Two Tone grabbed him by the collar, twisted, and slammed him into the wall. The suit wobbled. Two Tone repeated the motion three more times, denting the drywall. The suit fell limp and slid down to the floor.

Behind him, the other guard was also sprawled on the floor. Blood trickled out of his gut where a switchblade stuck out. Jet stood over the fallen thug rubbing his cut knuckles.

"Nothing I hate more than hounds pulling knives," Jet muttered.

The two flew down the dark basement halls. Screams, clatter, and chaos, continued above them. They whirled around the corner and into four more guards. They didn't see the pair coming until it was too late. Two Tone broke one punk's arm and coldcocked a second, and Jet rammed one's head into the wall and roundhouse kicked the last in one motion. They were already hitting the floor as the duo traversed the stairs.

The stairs led out into the backstage. Soundboards, lights, and folding chairs were strewn carefully about. The curtain was drawn and the band equipment was still set up though the band themselves were nowhere to be seen. The pair exited the stairs back out into the crowd.

It was a disaster. Two dozen mud monsters shuffled awkwardly across the dancefloor. Men and women, both adults and teenagers, were running around with no clear destination. Some of Stagger's grey suited men were fighting off the mud men with knives, bats, and pipes.

Two Tone growled. "Where is Sarpedon?"

"He might already be upstairs."

"No way." Two Tone ran straight for the stairs to the office. They slipped between mud men and thugs duking it out. One punk screamed as a claw slashed his wrist. "I hope Templeton plans on making his move soon."

Jet joined him as they ascended the stairs. "We might have a bigger problem than that."

In the hall ahead of them lay the bodies of six of Stagger's men. They were strewn all about the hall, and covered in blood. Some had crossbow bolts sticking out of them. Lightning from the large barred window flashed long shadows along the hall. Two Tone recognized a few of them.

"Look out, man," Steve-O rasped. He was lying against the wall. Slash marks ran along his chest up his face and across his forehead. "They ain't human."

Jet kneeled beside him. "Stay still. We'll get you some water later."

"What?" the injured man asked.

"I'll tell you when we get out. You can put in a good word with your sister for me."

"Take it." Steve-O handed Jet his wooden bat. "You're gonna need it, man. They ain't human."

Two Tone followed the kid's gaze along the hallway.

In front of the door to the office were two monsters. The first was Lorna holding the crossbow toward them and Jonelle around her neck. She had a bag by her side that looked to contain the crossbow bolts. Beside her was Graves holding the shirt collar of a man with a mangled face with blood pouring off of it.

Lorna snarled. "You're still alive?"

"Look out!" Jonelle shouted to him. "They're insane!"

"We were too slow," Jet muttered.

Graves spat on the red carpet and threw down the corpse. "I've been waiting for this."

Two Tone sneered. "This time I'll be a lot less gentle."

"These are the two you met in the apartment?" Jet asked. "They don't look like much."

"They're not." Two Tone let out a low laugh. "They just have a problem staying dead."

He held his smile in the face of the two aggressors despite the sight before him. The seven bodies splayed across the stained carpets had been sliced into and filled with holes. His guts tightened and he choked down some bile. They wouldn't get the fear they wanted from him.

But one body caught Two Tone's eye. There was a lone figure lying by the corner of the stairs—the one that almost got away. Eddie Masters had been slashed along the back and his throat was emptying out what little life remained. He had one hand to his neck and the other stretching out toward the stairs. Despite his efforts, his wide, still eyes clung to the simple reality that he wouldn't be getting away from this one. This was not where Eddie Masters was supposed to die.

Two Tone crouched down. He reached into Eddie's coat pocket and fished out the combat chain.

There was a flash out of the corner of his vision making him duck forward. A blade sliced against the back of his head. Hot liquid ran down his neck. Small hairs were cut loose. Beside him was Graves brandishing a knife. Drops of Two Tone's blood stained the blade. The gleam of the ceremonial knife matched Graves' maniacal grin as it plunged for Two Tone's throat.

At that moment, the yellow sparks of light returned. The world slowed to a crawl for a millisecond. A line of light passed before him.

The yellow sparks flickered from Graves' knife and connected to Two Tone's throat as if indicating the oncoming trajectory of the attack. His brain clicked obvious thoughts into place. This was where he was supposed to die. But the sparks were there to show him another way.

He flung his chain, but the angle was off. The weapon struck at air as the knife reached his neck. Cool steel tipped into his skin letting out lifeblood.

There was a crunch. Graves' neck bent awkwardly, and the knife skidded off Two Tone's throat. The Clay Man spun like a top into the left side wall and fell to one knee.

"What the hell was that, Two Tone?" Jet asked. He held the wooden bat tight. He stood before Two Tone with heavy breaths. His teeth were grinding together. "Did you see those sparks?"

"I did."

Two Tone jumped back up, he threw the brass knuckles to Jet who was much better with them. Jet pocketed them.

"That's no excuse for sloppiness. Did you come this far to die to Pawns when the King's ahead?"

All these years later and Two Tone was still being saved by Jet. The sparks flickered around Graves in a sort of skin of yellow light. The ball lightning had become a highlighter, showing Graves' breaths an instant before they came. Was it predicting his movements?

Across from the pair, Graves swore under his breath. He took hold of his head and gave it a sudden twist. The crack resulting was a sound the likes of Two Tone was familiar with. But it didn't kill the dreg. For some unfathomable reason, the neck had realigned with his spinal cord. He brandished two of his knives as fury broke out over him.

"Sparks?" the freak asked. "Are you idiots smoking some bad Rocks? Cutting them in glass? You should be careful who you buy from, ya?"

But Two Tone's concern laid elsewhere. "Where's Jonelle?"

At some point during the altercation, the woman had vanished, and Jonelle with her. Only Graves remained in the hall, holding his two ceremonial knives.

"Damn," Jet swore. "She was just here."

"Let's get this cat in a box and get moving." Two Tone wrapped his fingers around the chain and began spinning it. "I've had about enough of Sarpedon's crap to last me a millennia."

Graves tipped his hat forward with the edge of his left knife. His wound bled speckled spots of mud. Dark fissures spread from his neck up the side of his cheek to his greasy black hair. The dead men on the floor did succeed in wounding him—streaks of their blood may have stained his coat, but tiny piles of dust and black mud lay at his feet. His smile was stained black.

"You are wasting your time, cats." Graves gestured to the room behind him. "Even if you get into Stagger Lee's room, what do you think you'll be able to do? Sarpedon will eat your hearts."

Yellow lightning from the outside cast shadows across the corpses. The stink of ash from the dreg's open wounds strengthened. Floorboards creaked under the bloodstained carpet with every step Graves made.

Then, as if a fast forward button had been smashed, he lunged. The yellow lights pointed at his trajectory.

Both knives were aimed for Jet. Two Tone reached to his right and kicked his friend. The left knife slid along the former leader's side. A thin line of blood dripped from Jet's ripped suit, just missing slicing him open. Jet fell backwards.

Graves twisted his swing toward Two Tone. The maniac's right knife plunged into Two Tone's chest—but was caught in mid-thrust! The knife would not budge. Jet had grabbed hold as he fell, his coat jacket wrapped around Grave's appendage.

"What the hell?!" Graves shouted.

Two Tone threw his chain out. Grave's nose crumpled in a sickening crunch. Dark mud gushed from the wound.

Jet sprang back up with the bat in hand. He brought it against Graves' neck once, and then a second time. Graves roared, black blood spilling from his skin.

Then it happened. Lightning made the room, and Two Tone's path, clear for but a single instance. The trail highlighted his path.

Two Tone leaped on the maniac's back and wrapped his chain around the damaged neck. He pulled tight. Graves choked and tumbled backwards, slamming into drywall. Pieces of wall slashed against Two Tone's back. Graves growled as his throat cracked under the pressure. The maniac wobbled.

The bat held tight, Jet swung for Graves' knees. The crack reverberated through the hall. Graves dropped to the floor face first, with Two Tone still clinging to his back.

"Now!" Two Tone yelled.

Jet swung his bat into the window. The first hit only cracked it, and the second did the same. The third strike hit its mark. The windswept downpour sprayed the glass downwards. Two Tone winced as glass landed in his back and around him. Rainwater dumped in chunks over the carpet.

Jet jumped backwards, tumbling over a corpse and hitting the floor. The bat slid across the soaked carpet.

The rain burned into Graves, melting the flesh from his exposed wounds, but it didn't slow him down. He leaped up, throwing his neck back, knocking Two Tone loose. The former punk tumbled back into the shattered drywall, dropping his chain.

Steam smoked from Graves' open wounds and bent neck, but his teeth remained clenched. He turned on Two Tone, both knives searching for blood.

Two Tone tried to stand. His back was on fire, and his vision fuzzed. Fresh blood was forming under his bandages. Fiery pain shot through his legs.

The maniac moved forward for the kill, and Two Tone slid up against the wall.

Knives plunged for his chest, and Two Tone slid downward. The knives stabbed drywall. Two Tone sprang up on burning legs and wrapped his left arm around the attacker's outstretched limbs. Graves was locked in place with his arms seized. Two Tone brought his right elbow forward and slammed it into Graves' nose. The strike loosened bloodstained teeth.

Jet finally stood up once more and swung the bat against the monster's back. The wood split. A watery bellow escaped from Graves. His jaw steamed and dislocated. It crashed against the wet carpet. The storm had softened his flesh.

With a burst of strength, Graves broke Two Tone's grip. As the punk reeled, Graves captured Two Tone's shoulder and spun. He let go, and whipped Two Tone loose. He spun through the hall like a human wheel. He skidded to a stop on the stained carpet near the end of the hall. Two Tone struggled up to his elbows.

Graves turned, and Jet moved in again. The monster roared at his enemy, and Graves ran a knife into his chest.

It did not pierce all the way, but it did cut. Jet held the attacking arm tight, his feet sliding on the carpet against the force. The second knife went for him, but his speed was dulled. Jet brought the broken bat up and smashed into Graves' left arm, severing the soft appendage and leaving the bat shattered. The left limb spun through the air and touched down in a cold puddle on the floor two feet before Two Tone. He used the moment to pry the knife from the detached arm. Jet ducked back to the carpet, dodging the next swing. His chest wound was bleeding through his suit.

Graves' glanced at his missing arm, eyes wide. Black blood coated him. His shock slid to seething rage when he spotted Two Tone finally standing up again.

"Goodbye, Graves," muttered Two Tone. He wobbled on his feet. Searing pain pushed against him. "Sarpedon will be joining you soon."

Graves screamed and thundered toward Two Tone, his cracked and crumbling face red with rage.

The steam evaporated with Graves' flesh and bone as he ran forward. Two Tone brought Grave's dropped knife forward, but the maniac didn't notice. He lifted Two Tone with his charge.

As he was lifted from the ground, Two Tone plunged the ceremonial knife into Graves' neck. Mud spurted from the wound. Even though he continued stabbing, Graves kept charging.

Wood crunched and splintered behind Two Tone's back. The hallway door had broken open.

Two Tone swiped one last time with the knife, and Graves' head spun off his shoulders. The pair hit the floor against the broken door fragments. Blood leaked from Two Tone's wounds.

The maniac's body twitched on the floor. The steam had won. Graves' remains disintegrated into the ether. Fierce eyes on the decapitated head watched his prey before finally rolling back and letting death take it. Graves wouldn't be getting up from that one.

Behind him, there was a scream.

He spun on his knees and leaped up, still sore from the last attack. His muscles strained against him.

At the end of the office stood Lorna holding Jonelle by her hair with her crossbow in hand, and Stagger Lee in the chair at his desk, his teeth clenched. Behind the chair, with his hands on Stagger's shoulders, stood Sarpedon.

"You know," the big man said. "There are few things more annoying than splinters. They take so much time to dig out, and they never stop irritating until they are removed. And you, Two Tone, are the single most annoying splinter I have ever had the misfortune of pulling out."

Two Tone smiled, tasting blood. "Story of my life."

Chapter 12
"The Immortal Eyes of the Moons"

The four figures in the room looked upon the bloody form of Two Tone like he was a ghost. Truth be told, he wasn't far off from becoming one. Their mouths agape, Sarpedon and Lorna spared glances at each other. Stagger Lee's lip quivered slightly. Only Jonelle cracked a smile at Two Tone's unbelievable entrance.

"Back so soon?" she asked.

He chuckled. "Women. Never enough, is it?"

The office was the same as before, except the black curtains had been torn from the window. The window was covered in cracks as if someone had smashed it deliberately. It probably had something to do with Stagger's shivering.

"Two Tone!" Stagger cried out like a madman. Everyone in the room turned to the man. "Please calm yourself. You've done enough damage! There is a way we can work all this out that will be beneficial to all of us—you, our friends, your girl . . ."

"The same girl you tried to give up to these hounds?"

Two Tone spat blood on the carpet. "You're juggling too many chainsaws, Stagger. The chances of you making it out of here with functioning organs are lower than me just turning around and walking out. I'm not even talking about what *he'll* do to you. Get it yet?"

Stagger wiped his pudgy brow with a wrinkly pocket handkerchief. Even after so many years, the grease ball had never shown so much as a sweat drop around others. He was always in control. Yet, as Sarpedon in his far less impressive black suit and matching tie clapped his stiff manicured hands on Stagger's shoulders, the thug couldn't help but jump. He forced a smile as his fingers twitched on the desk.

"We can work this out. Right, Sarpedon?"

Sarpedon's thin smile over his smooth cheeks remained as cool as ever. The lack of creases on his skin betrayed his natural menace. Maybe it was why Stagger thought he had a chance.

"What was our deal, Mr. Lee?" Sarpedon asked. His chilled tone could have frozen water. "You killed 'ol Billy, scared the living daylights out of this city's trash, and became a legend. You've had years to live off this junk empire. Don't you feel it's time you gave what you owe?"

Stagger bit his lip. "All you did was take the gun!"

"And I incinerated the bullet in his body!" Sarpedon roared. He wheeled around in front of Stagger Lee's chair and gripped him by the throat. "You pride-filled fool. I made you. Without me you would still be an errand boy for Luciano!"

Stagger fought for composure. "What do you want?"

"What do I—" Sarpedon stopped himself.

He released his victim's throat, and straightened the suit collar he had just ruffled. The rage rolling off him died in an instant.

"You've had your time, Mr. Lee. Our blood pact must be fulfilled. It's time for you to give me what you owe me. Now don't fuss, please. This has gone on long enough. I could always take you back to that harbor instead. That was the other option. Do you prefer death? You really are a sad, little man, Lee."

Stagger's chair jumped back as he stood up. He gestured to the large seat. "You can have Cordova. I only ever wanted to be your second. Really."

"*Really?*"

He nodded. "Really."

Sarpedon nodded back and stroked his own smooth chin. "Impressive, Mr. Lee. I accept. So here is your first duty as my second."

"Yes, sir?"

"Join me."

Stagger looked at him sideways, and then his eyes bulged. He stood in place as his whole body shook. He was like one possessed. His legs began to move on their own toward Sarpedon. Every stepped jerked forward as the big man opened his arms as if for a great hug.

Two Tone was instantly reminded of what happened in the warehouse. What did Sarpedon actually do to Turk? Jonelle shivered as she looked on.

"No!" Stagger screamed. His head shook like a mental

patient. Some force was controlling his movements. "I know what you'll do. I've seen it. I'm not going in there. No! I'd rather . . . I'd . . . I'd . . ."

There wasn't a second's hesitation. Stagger Lee bit down on his left hand, and screamed. He broke the skin and whatever appeared to be controlling his movements. In his rage, he swooped toward the window overlooking his club, his limbs fighting. Saliva pooled in the corners of his chubby lips.

He ran and jumped through the cracked window, limbs flailing. Glass showered over him. He twisted as he fell through the air, madness spewing from his mouth. Two Tone couldn't see from the angle, but the thud was loud enough to tell him what he already knew. Stagger Lee was dead.

Sarpedon looked down from the broken glass and sighed. "That was a shame. I gave him that mud years back, and this is how he repays me? He would rather die than serve me. I was only trying to save him."

With the monster's back turned, Two Tone tried to make his move. His throbbing thigh made him stop in his tracks and wooziness overtook him momentarily. He readied the knife he had taken from Graves.

"Stop moving!" Lorna shouted to the girl.

Jonelle wrestled and twisted around her captor's hold. In her escape attempt, she met the back of the monster woman's hand. Jonelle hit the floor with a thump.

"Damn bitch." Lorna towered over her victim. "What do you think you're doing?"

"I've seen enough of this," Jonelle replied. Tears had begun to trickle down her cheeks. "No more killing. This is too much. Haven't you done enough?"

Lorna chuckled. "Where do think we are? Earth? This isn't paradise—not yet. Once Sarpedon finishes—"

The words seized in her mouth. Lorna felt at her throat for the cause of the disturbance. That was when she finally noticed the thrown knife plunged into her neck. Two Tone had hit his mark. Steam burst from the wound, and she dropped her crossbow to the ground. Bolts from her bag clattered to the floor as she weaved.

"Sarpedon *is* finished," Two Tone said. That was a throw to make Jet proud.

"Masterful toss," Jet said.

Jet emerged from the doorway clutching his stomach and limping. Beside him was Steve-O leaning on his left. It was difficult to tell who was supporting who. They were both torn and ragged.

"Speak of the devil," Two Tone whispered.

Lorna fell forward, but Jonelle sprang up in a rage. With a thrust of her palm she knocked the knife upward and through the monster's throat. Clay skin shattered. Lorna's head popped off her shoulders in a shower of chips and dust. Black blood squirted loose as the body slumped to the floor. Her head rolled to a stop at Sarpedon's feet.

Sarpedon's expression remained stony. He took one step towards Jonelle, and then another. "That was unnecessary. We were talking peacefully. I understand Mr. Lee overreacted—"

"Stay back." Two Tone stepped in front of the girl. The

knife dripped black blood as he held it toward Sarpedon. He spoke to Jonelle over his shoulder. "You and Jet need to get out of here. This one is all mine."

"You're leaving a girl with me?" Jet asked. He slid in beside Two Tone, still leaning on Steve-O. "Boy, you've changed."

"I'm with you, man," Steve-O said. "But you got to promise to show me how to throw like that."

Jet smiled through his bloody lips. "It's all about spacing."

"Excuse me, gentlemen," Sarpedon said. "I believe we were talking. What you did to Lorna was superfluous. I expected better from you, Ms. Verdant. You are not the brute these punks are."

"Oh, shut your mouth." Two Tone scooped up the fallen crossbow and bag off the carpet. "We both know she's not dead. I don't know what you cats are, but I do know a lot of water is the only thing that stops you from getting back up."

Sarpedon smiled and shrugged. "Yes . . . and no. Those shells you destroy can only be obliterated through large quantities of water infecting the interior. But they don't die—they return to me. I do not even need you to kill Lorna to explain it. Watch and learn, punks."

Sarpedon crouched down and lifted Lorna's decapitated head up. With a sentence that sounded like backwards speech, he crushed the skull in his fingers. As before, steam burst from the broken clay and wafted into the air.

"Did you see that?" Sarpedon asked with a smile. "She is now one with me! My minions return to dust to become my bones. I can then cast them out again to make them whole when I so desire. They live forever."

"Mary, Mother of God," Two Tone said in an odd moment of petition. "You actually did kill them, didn't you?"

Sarpedon's stare deadened as his square head slanted. His smile died.

Jonelle grabbed Two Tone's shoulder. "What are you talking about?"

"They were all already dead. Graves, Lorna, the ones at the warehouse . . . Sarpedon killed them. His ability is to give life to clay dolls. I don't know where he got it or how he is able to do it, but he does not turn people into Clay Men. He imprints their personalities—their brainwaves into those dolls. That has to be it. Those things we saw were not people, or even transformed humans. They weren't real to begin with."

"Admirable guess." Sarpedon let his disdain simmer on his response. "But you are wrong. I preserve them wholesale within myself. This is why you should consider my offer. Don't you see? Without me, you will all eventually die and be forgotten. I offer immortality! Real invincibility. No more pain; no more death. No more sickness, starvation, or fear. What the hell is wrong with any of that?"

That was when Two Tone noticed an odd movement on Sarpedon's large frame. Through the suit were tiny ripples of obscure patterns. After a hard look he began to make them out—faces. Horrendous expressions of fear and pain filled the contours of their visages. One of them he recognized as Lazlo, and another was Lorna. Sweat trickled down Two Tone's neck.

"So you see?" Sarpedon bellowed. "I am your savior."

Jet slipped on the brass knuckles from his pocket. "Some of us don't want to be immortal. Hell, I don't even want to reach thirty. I've gotten enough fun for one lifetime."

"If that's all you want, Sarpedon," Two Tone said, aiming the crossbow, "I can send you to a place filled with people just like you."

"You're small time thinkers, all of you!" Sarpedon roared. "They all live on inside of me where I can endlessly offer them new shells to inhabit. I cannot touch or change their souls; I merely allow them a place to rest. They will always return to me. They can never die."

"But *you* will." Two Tone spat more blood on the carpet. His head beat like a snare drum.

"Did our previous encounter teach you nothing? You cannot kill me. Please. Violence solves nothing. Grow some semblance of a brain, Two Tone, and learn to think like an adult."

"Okay," Two tone replied.

The trigger squeezed, and the first bolt flew through the air. It landed in Sarpedon's neck. The monster fell back a step, surprised at the insolence. Two Tone loaded and fired the next bolt and then the next. The bolts pierced Sarpedon's chest and skull.

Sarpedon blandly stared to Two Tone, and then the approaching figure on his right.

Jet rammed his brass knuckles into Sarpedon's face. The monster spun, and Jet brandished a knife from his belt. It was Graves' second blade. He jabbed it into Sarpedon's back, and twisted.

He whispered into Sarpedon's ear. "When you see him, tell Stagger I'm gonna burn the Rabid Rabbit down with his corpse."

Jet booted Sarpedon in the chest. The monster stumbled backwards out the broken glass of the overlooking window. The big man soared through the club and crashed down to the floor below. The resulting thud somehow didn't shake the building.

Jet slumped back against the desk. He clutched his stomach. "I think I overdid it."

Jonelle ran over and pushed her hands down on the wound. He was turning ghost white. Steve-O returned to his side, helping her with the stab wound.

"Yeah, you did," Two Tone said. He retrieved the knife that had been used against Lorna. "Looks like I'm going to have to get down there and make sure he doesn't get back up."

Gunshots erupted from the floor below. Alarms went off blocks away from the police station.

Two Tone shook his head. "Too late."

Chain in hand, Two Tone sprinted down the stairs and to the concert floor. He hoped his second wind would not give out. The crowds of people had evacuated, but the building was not barren.

Broken tables and rubble littered the open floor. There were shredded bodies of Stagger's men and a bunch of punks dressed in dark clothes. Piles of mud were splashed everywhere like an abstract expressionist painting. The only Clay Man still standing was Sarpedon, surrounded by the surviving punks in black clothes and a handful of Stagger's goons. The monster was bleeding black blood through his cuts and punctured holes, and his left arm was bent at the wrong angle. The eight remaining members of the crowd looked just as beat up.

From the back of the crowd stepped Templeton. He still wore the black suit that moved over his cut up body. Sarpedon smiled at the younger suit as the bolts fell out of his wounds.

"Very impressive, Templeton," Sarpedon said. He nodded like a proud father. "I didn't think you would ever gain this level of support. I apologize for crushing the boy's throat over there. He really should have been more careful when checking on me."

Over by Stagger lay a body mere foot from him. Two Tone recognized it as one of the punks who met him in Templeton's group. It was the kid wearing the green cap and the oddly psychedelic shirt. He wouldn't be getting up again.

Templeton bared his teeth. "This has been going on long enough, hasn't it? Isn't it time to finally give it up? This planet is almost entirely water—your puppets can't live here. Neither can you. This was always a fool's errand, Sarpedon."

"We can create our own rain." Sarpedon waved a dismissive hand at the half-dead punks. "We can run our own generators. We don't need the sun; we don't need the sky, or the moons. Once we cover the Central with our own ceiling to block out Achaea's rain, we can create a world inside. We can correct the mistakes of those solipsists who left their children behind to die in this dusty corner of the universe. You can live forever. I don't understand why neither you nor Two Tone over there understands any of this."

"You gave me this suit," Templeton said. "Because you said I was too weak to ingest the mud. You said it would give me strength; that I could cut my own path. My dad used to say that the suit makes the man."

"He was a smart man. But you couldn't swallow the mud, so how else could I gift you, Lennox? Your skin is a weapon. You can cut through anything. No one can stand against you. I fail to see the issue."

Templeton lifted a hand forward. The black suit rippled and bubbled like a cauldron. A tar claw slid from the fabric and swiped at the air, breaking a nearby table to pieces.

"You fail to see much, Sarpedon. This suit prevents me. It prevents me from sleeping; it urges me to devour. This is no gift. My father would see me for the monster I am now."

"No, that's where you're wrong!" Sarpedon's tone brightened. "He is very proud of you, Lennox. He tells me every single day about what a strong boy he has. You don't underst—"

Lennox Templeton burst forward, and plunged his bladed arms into Sarpedon's chest. The suit itself lashed out like a wild beast, clawing up Sarpedon like a Lion's prey. Black blood sprayed from the openings like a geyser. The suit rippled and thrashed off Templeton's body as if in a rage. Swaths of Sarpedon's flesh were torn free.

"You really don't understand, boy."

As if hitting a stone wall, the suit then lost all momentum. It took a moment for the room to realize what was happening. Templeton was not slicing Sarpedon apart—the suit was being slurped like a spaghetti dinner. Within a second the suit had been ripped clean of its host. All that remained was Templeton's pale, sickly white body standing naked on the dancefloor.

"Well," Sarpedon said with a sigh. "If this is what you'd prefer, you can die now."

Naked Templeton dropped to the bloody dance floor. He did not move again.

Black blood poured from Sarpedon's ripped flesh. His breaths fell heavy, his right eye was missing, and his left arm barely clung to his body, but his smile remained. He was still in control, even if Templeton's hits were not completely in vain. Despite Sarpedon looking more like a torn apart gazelle than he did a carnivore, none of the eight thugs still standing would approach. He turned on his heel toward the emergency exit and thundered away.

Two Tone watched dumbfounded as Templeton and Stagger's men stood still, unable to move.

"Is anyone going to stop him?" Two Tone asked.

No one spoke. They all slunk to the floor as if their wounds were too much. Even A-Rail leaned against a battered stone pillar, his pipe in one hand and clutching his chest with the other. He glanced at Two Tone, but only shook his head.

Two Tone slid beside Templeton, and crouched over. The kid was barely breathing. "I need someone to wait for the cops outside. Tell them to send in the paramedics. The rest of us will go after Sarpedon."

None replied. They were still looking after the quickly

escaping Sarpedon. A-Rail silently regarded their fallen leader but he also did not move. The door to the exit closed, and Sarpedon was gone. A heavy atmosphere of defeat remained in his wake.

"Hello?" Two Tone shouted at the surrounding crowd. "Are you listening?"

"We hear you," Jet rasped.

Behind him, Jet, Steve-O, and Jonelle, descended the stairs to the bottom floor. He was wobbling, but still barely holding together leaning on the kid.

"Go get him," Jonelle said. She threw him his chain. "We'll take care of things here."

"Don't make me regret saving your ass," Jet added.

"Jet!" A-Rail muttered.

"Come on, Two Tone." Jet gestured to the other punks. "You're the only cat here who can still catch him. These idiots aren't going to budge. They've already given up."

Two Tone took one last look at the group of punks, but none of them moved. With the strength remaining in his legs, he pressed onward with slow steps. His muscles screamed out, and his chest was growing tight. Blood dripped from his wounds as he approached the exit door.

"Wait!" A-Rail called out. "Are you crazy? Didn't you see what he just did to Templeton?"

"I did. And?"

"I thought you might have grown up, Two Tone. We're not kids anymore; this isn't the old days. You can't keep running into fights hoping that things work out. Sarpedon will kill you."

"Probably."

"I thought you just wanted a quiet life away from this sort of thing. If you go after him now, he'll kill you. Think for once. It's over. He'll probably die in the rain."

Jet laughed at his former subordinate. "You were always such a snake, A-Rail. Never there when we need you; always fighting battles that you know you'll win. Why else would you sign up with that cat on the floor over there? What did you think we were fighting back in the day for? To rule Cordova? To get rich? All we wanted was to be left alone. And this is where we are now."

"But if he goes after Sarpedon now, he'll die."

"I know," Two Tone interrupted. "But so will Sarpedon. If I don't stop him now, he's just going to come back again. The rain isn't enough to end him. I know it."

The crowd stayed silent as he pushed against the heavy metal door. Two Tone caught one last glance from Jonelle, her perfect slender form burned into his bones and memories. He craved one last embrace; even one more sniff of her fragrance would have been enough. But he couldn't stop now.

He swung open the emergency exit, and stepped out into the downpour of the night.

Sirens and barking dogs from blocks away awaited him. He was surrounded by rain soaked trash and cement. The downpour swallowed him as arcs of lightning flashed overhead.

Dozens of bodies in suits and black clothing lay about in the alley, some breathing, among piles of mud staining the concrete and brick walls. A wooden bat lay in a puddle, and he took it up. His tired legs shuffled through the alley into the abandoned street. In the alley ahead he spotted Sarpedon limping into the next alley.

"Hey, cat!" Two Tone shouted. "Where you going at this hour?"

Sarpedon froze, and glanced back. His coal black eyes could have ignited a bonfire.

The cold wind whistled through the metal scaffolding and pools of water from the overturned trash lids blew across Two Tone's face. He wiped it clean with the back of his bloody hand. This would be it. He made a mental note of the knife behind his back, the bat in hand, and the chain in his pocket. He would need them all to even stand a chance.

The Clay Man flinched in the howling wind. "You really are a bug, Two Tone."

Two Tone limped a few more feet. "I prefer to think of myself as a cockroach. White-Haired Wolf was never a good name for me."

"You certainly have the brains to match such an insignificant insect. Do you realize that I have hundreds in here with me?" He rammed a fist to his stained chest and dark mud squirted free. "They are all in here waiting to be given life again. You are holding them back."

"I figure I'm doing them all a favor by smashing your skull like a grapefruit. I don't know who you are, or where you came from, but I know where I'm sending you. This town—this planet—will be much better off."

"This planet?" Sarpedon waved his crumpled hand

around the empty alley. "Just look around at this mess. I'm the only chance you have of escaping it."

"Abandonment theory, huh?" Two Tone sighed. Defeatists loved talking about how their ancestors were so stupid that they abandoned paradise on Earth. "Look, I don't know why we left Earth. Maybe it was perfect, and the colonists were horrible people who abandoned it for no reason except to screw us. Maybe there are people still there. Hell, maybe there are colonists on other worlds. I don't know; I don't care."

"Are you mad? Look at your city! I didn't do this. How many years have you been fighting to change it? And what was the result? I can make sure nothing like this ever happens again."

"And what about cats like me?"

"Devils can't be saved," Sarpedon said. "But if this is what you want then so be it. Never say that I am not a gracious god. I will find others."

"No, you won't."

"And you're going to stop me? The myth of Alexander the Great makes a good bedtime story, but I can make that myth real. I can conquer and hold this world. Why? Because they have nothing else to bind them. They need me. You think you can take on a god with a bat?"

"Philosophy can't stop anything, but a bat to the teeth can."

Sarpedon ran his fingers across his smooth face as if wiping dirt away. "If you insist."

Then, as if the heavens were parting, the rain simply

stopped. Both Sarpedon and Two Tone flinched. Up above where the nimbus clouds parted and broke, the light of the moons forced their way through. The wind continued unabated and howled like a scream. Except that it literally *was* a scream. It was Sarpedon.

Sarpedon charged through the alley, spit slobbering out the corners of his mouth, his eyes bulged and red as he fell upon Two Tone. The breeze was overtaken by his mindless ravings. His right fist clenched and his left arm flapping in the gust, Two Tone readied himself.

"Devil!" Sarpedon screamed.

Two Tone side-stepped and Sarpedon swung past. He swung the bat, cracking against the monster's left arm. The weakened limb detached and spun before landing on the drenched pavement. Sarpedon toppled sideways, slamming into trash cans. The monster was slower, but not slow enough. Only Two Tone's sixth sense saved his throat from splitting.

Dizziness threatened to overtake him. Two Tone's shoulders ached from the swing. He blinked the stars out of his vision. Blood trickled from the corners of his mouth.

Sarpedon slowly rose from the garbage.

"Devil," he muttered.

The bat descended on the monster. Sarpedon brought his right arm up and the weapon cracked open. Wood splinters sprayed out. Bits lodged into Two Tone's hands, arms, and cheeks. Sarpedon kicked his midsection, sending him backwards. Two Tone slammed against the wall.

"Nothing but a devil."

"I heard you the first two times." Two Tone's hands shook as he pulled splinters from his upper arms. His muscles strained as the blood leaked. "If I knew you weren't going to shut up I would have crushed your voice box first."

"You'll never escape. *Never.*"

"What? Cordova?"

"The shadows will eat all. They're always watching and licking their lips for their next meal. I can see them. I always see them. They won't let you leave."

"I can help your head leave your shoulders. What do the shadows have to say about that?"

Sarpedon moved like a sprinter. Two Tone's legs fought against him, preventing a dodge. Cold fingers clasped around Two Tone's throat and tightened. The former punk wheezed and gasped.

"Stop talking," Sarpedon whispered. "Listen to the shadows. They're laughing."

Darkness enclosed on Two Tone. Sparks popped before him as the night overtook all.

Sarpedon growled. "You can see them now."

A flash of electricity jolted Two Tone awake and reminded him. The knife! He slipped his cut right hand behind his back. Whatever that yellow lightning was, it knew how to get his attention. His left hand uselessly clasped Sarpedon's remaining arm.

Sarpedon's hollow laugh overtook his rage. "Even cockroaches eventually get squashed."

Two Tone swung his right arm upward. The knife jammed into Sarpedon's wrist, piercing right through. Black mud stained his jacket and sprayed over Two Tone's bloodstained face. Laughs became screams.

The grip around Two Tone's throat loosened and he slumped to the pavement. He held strong on his knees, and then slowly found himself sliding to the warm pavement. Sarpedon howled into the night.

Calm slumber comforted Two Tone, soothing his thoughts. Eternity was one sleep away. Finally, it was over.

In the corner of the dark, a sliver of light cracked like lightning in an overcast sky. Then he remembered it all. He remembered *her*.

He punched his cheek. Focus momentarily returned. His knees cracked as he stood, and his right hand went for his pocket. This was his last weapon. He made one last push for Sarpedon.

The chain lashed. He spun like a dancer, letting his blows fly. The weight of the chain crashed into Sarpedon, crunching skin. One of the strikes sent white teeth out into a nearby puddle. Sarpedon responded with a kick rocking against Two Tone's ribs and letting him cough blood.

Two Tone bounded forward against the hit, and ducked around a backhand. The chain swung out around Sarpedon's throat. Two Tone ducked behind him, back to back, holding each end of the weapon. Sarpedon struggled to grip the chain, his one remaining hand unable to close with a knife sticking through it. Two Tone leaned forward, lifting Sarpedon off the ground onto his back. His knees screamed and began to buckle.

"Takes more than that to kill a cockroach," Two Tone

rasped. His stomach burned and his back flared. "Next time use a bigger boot."

The monster struggle. Sarpedon's elbow cracked against Two Tone's ribs once more. Two Tone's knees gave. Then a sickening crack followed.

Sarpedon slumped, and Two Tone lost his balance. Both tipped to the cement, landing in a nearby puddle. Two Tone choked as water splashed up his nose. His stinging arms pulled him across the cement to the opposite wall. When he finally turned back he saw an unexpected sight.

The monster lay motionless in the water staring up at the sky. The knife was still in his wrist, his wounds leaked mud, and his neck was jagged at a wrong angle. Steam gushed from his raw lacerations.

"Damn moons," he growled. "Always watching. Devils. *Killers.*"

Sarpedon's clay merged into mud which was absorbed by the puddle and faded away.

Two Tone fell silent against the wall. Not even his fingers would budge. His arms were heavier than ten tons, and his legs numbed. Breaths arrived heavy and hard. If only he could have held her once more. There was nothing left for him but her.

There in the sky were the two moons looking down on Achaea like a sidelong glance through the dark. They were eerie, despite being totally natural. They watched him as he blinked one last time and fell into slumber.

*

Several times Two Tone awoke. How many times, he couldn't tell. Once, his phone rang. He dug it out and answered, unable to say but one word or even look down at it. But he heard every word the speaker said.

"*You've done well, Mr. Fisher.*"

Two Tone's finger slid toward ending the call.

"*This will be the last time you hear from me,*" Green Eyes said. "*I only wanted to thank you for saving my daughter.*"

He blinked. Jonelle's mother had a talent, but she never said what it was. Did it continue after death? Maybe she had one of those rumored abilities. There was certainly much more to this world than he thought. What else was hiding on this shadow planet?

"*I am out of time. Please look after Jonelle in my stead. And goodbye, Two Tone.*"

There was a large burst of static. Then the line went dead. And so the darkness returned.

*

"Henry," Jonelle said.

Two Tone blinked awake. His head was resting on Jonelle's lap. She was looking down on him, tears in her eyes but a beatific smile highlighting everything that drove him crazy about her. Her soft touch warmed his tender wounds. Small raindrops fell upon her hair and dripped down to his bloodied face, carrying her scent with it.

She held back a sob. "You're alive."

He nodded as best he could. "I am."

"I'm sorry I put you through all this." She gestured

around her. All he could make out were flashing lights and sirens. He heard chatter. Cops. "Looks like we won't get that dance after all."

"What happened?" he rasped out.

"Jet and Templeton are on the way to the hospital. Templeton's gang was also brought in."

"And?"

"I talked with some of the officers—did you know that Jet worked with them? He used his connections with Stagger to keep track of his dealings. Steve-O's brother is an officer—that's apparently where Jet first got in touch with them. Your friends are strange birds. Anyway, these officers going to take us in and ask some questions, but we should be okay. There's no gun, bullet, or victim, from the harbor, so there's no charge against us. We won't have to spend the rest of our days in separate cells."

"Don't care about cops." He took a deep breath. "Don't care about dancing. Come across the sea with me. We'll go to the frontier together, get out of this place."

She laughed. "Boy, you work fast. We haven't even had a dance yet."

"I'll settle for a date."

"You will?"

"For now. How about this?"

Two Tone reached up, his arm in spasm, and ran his fingers through her silk-soft copper hair. He pressed his palm against her cheek, and then the base of her neck. With his last strength, he pulled her tight close into an embrace. Her warmth chased the cold from his damp bones as her breath met his. Their lips touched and with that so did the world around them grow brighter. She squeezed in tighter as he pressed against her.

Eventually, they parted, but only by an inch.

"That," she said, "I like."

"I knew you would."

He thought he saw something out of the corner of his eye moving in the alley. It flashed like ball lightning. His head swirled as sleep attacked his thoughts. Police aside, they were alone in the alley. The presence had departed.

There were no monsters left in the dark of Cordova. Only one animal remained in the periphery of his vision leaping across the rain bedecked balconies. He knew it well. It was only a cat.

About J.D. Cowan

J.D. Cowan is a writer with an obsession for stories and Truth. He takes pleasure in looking for Light in the places where darkness grips the tightest.

His works include the young adult novel "*Knights of the End*" and short stories in "*Superheroes: The Crossover Alliance Volume 3*" by the Crossover Alliance, the PulpRev Sampler, and "*Paragons*" by Silver Empire. He blogs about stories and entertainment at wastelandandsky.blogspot.ca and can be found on Twitter @wastelandJD for those interested.

www.ingramcontent.com/pod-product-compliance
Lightning Source LLC
Chambersburg PA
CBHW060815120626
46557CB00001B/221